A DREAM OF ...HING

Appearing in an English translation for the first time, A DREAM OF SOMETHING is Pasolini's pastoral novel, an evocative picture of life in a part of Italy which held bitter-sweet memories for him. Friuli is located near the borders of Yugoslavia and Austria. It was here that his mother had been born, making the place intensely special for the young Pasolini who was bound to her by an obsessive love. His first published work was a volume of verse in the dialect of Friuli, and it was here that mother and son lived as evacuees during the Second World War. His first sexual experiences were with the local boys, and the future of the region was something which fired his political imagination and led him to join the Communist Party in 1947.

The novel is set in 1948, and though versions of the work date from that time, the book appeared in 1962 after the appearance and scandalous literary success of *Ragazzi di vita* (1955) and *A Violent Life* (1959). Where those novels are concerned with the young in the slums on the edge of Rome, A DREAM OF SOMETHING deals with the youths such as Pasolini had known and been drawn to in the small towns, villages and hamlets of Friuli. Episodic in technique, the story concerns three boys looking for work, who lead lives of dancing on Sundays, drinking wine and making music, cycling around the countryside and generally experiencing the pleasures and pains of love, as well as the sorrow of death. The demonstration in 1948 (based on an actual event) is presented as a moment of historical and personal truth, one in which the political fervour of the Left is exalted and ritualized through a passionate physical clash with the guardians of bourgeois justice. It is in the savage poetry of a death that the lives and aspirations of these Friulians are enriched.

PIER PAOLO PASOLINI

Pasolini is one of the most widely acclaimed artists of the twentieth century. He is known primarily for the films he began making in the 1960s, the most famous of which are *The Gospel According to St Matthew*, *Teorema*, *The Decameron*, *The Canterbury Tales*, *Arabian Nights* and *Salò*. He was also a remarkable poet, and won fame and notoriety with his two Roman novels, *Ragazzi di vita* and *Una vita violenta*. In 1975 he was murdered by a homosexual prostitute.

PIER PAOLO PASOLINI

A Dream of Something

Translated from the Italian and
with an Introduction by
STUART HOOD

QUARTET ENCOUNTERS

Quartet Books London New York

First published in English in Great Britain by
Quartet Books Limited, 1988
A member of the Namara Group
27/29 Goodge Street, London W1P 1FD
First published in Italian as *Il Sogno di una Cosa* by
Garzanti Editore Copyright © by Garzanti Editore s.p.a.,
1962, 1970, 1987
Translation Copyright © 1988 by Stuart Hood
Introduction Copyright © 1988 by Stuart Hood

British Library Cataloguing in Publication Data

Pasolini, Pier Paolo, *1922–1975*
   A dream of something.
   I. Title   II. Il sogno di una cosa.
   English
   853′.914[F]
   0 7043 0048 6

Typeset by MC Typeset Limited, Chatham, Kent
Printed and bound in Great Britain at
The Camelot Press plc, Southampton

Introduction

Friuli is part of that region of Italy which borders on Yugoslavia and Austria. It is traversed by the Tagliamento river which from the Carnic Alps in the north runs down through the battlefields of World War I to the Adriatic. The setting of much of *A Dream of Something* is the countryside on the right bank of the Tagliamento. Of its peasant inhabitants Pasolini wrote that their destiny for five centuries had been 'to work, pray, suffer and die'. Here Pasolini's mother, to whom he was bound by an obsessive love, was born into a family established for hundreds of years in the little town of Casarsa. It was here that he and his mother – his father, whom he detested, was a British prisoner-of-war in Kenya – lived as evacuees during World War II; here that he had his first sexual experiences with local boys; here that he produced his first published work, a volume of verse in the dialect of Friuli, which caused an academic scandal because it employed – as he put it – words which 'in all the centuries of their use had never been written'. It was to Casarsa that he returned after the armistice of September 1943 and the disbandment of the Italian army, in which he had served for only a week. In Casarsa he lived under Mussolini's puppet Republic of Salò (which would give its name to his last, terrifying film) and saw his younger brother leave to join the partisans in the mountains and die in the internecine quarrels between rebel bands of different political loyalties. Pasolini himself took no active part in the Resistance. His political ideas were still forming. Catholicism continued to have a strong emotional hold on him although he had grown disillusioned with the Church. He was concerned about the future of Friuli, its political and cultural autonomy, which Fascism had refused to acknowledge and of which language was an important expression, and about the threat of Yugoslav ambitions in this border area. When he did make a political decision, however, it led him in 1947 to join the Communist Party, although it was by pro-Yugoslav Communist partisans that his brother had been killed only two years before. By 1949 he was a branch secretary and a delegate to the Paris Peace Congress.

By this time he was teaching boys in a school in Valvasone. It was not his first experience as a teacher, for during the war he had set up a private school in Casarsa for a group of young people whom he fired with his enthusiasm for dialect and its use in literature. With some of them he had founded an Academy of the Friulian Language. Now as a state employee he continued to pursue the same interests and to deploy his extraordinary and highly unorthodox educational skills. Meantime he was deeply involved in politics, taking a line that deviated from the Communist Party's in the debate over autonomy for Friuli, which the Christian Democrats supported for deeply conservative reasons and the Communists opposed out of solidarity with the Yugoslavs. His description of conditions in Yugoslavia in the first episode of *A Dream of Something* can be read as a reflection of his political reservations about Communism in that country just as his picture of Swiss life in a latter episode expresses his criticism of an acquisitive society. This was a period when the inadequacy of government measures, as formulated in the de Gasperi decree, to alleviate the effects of the war and unemployment on the peasantry led in 1948 to demonstrations involving police and troops – events that form a central episode in *A Dream of Something*, in which Pasolini makes clear his stance on domestic politics. Meantime his reputation as a poet was growing; he was successfully entering those competitions for literary prizes which were such an important feature in Italian intellectual life. He was also reflecting on the role of the writer in society and coming to conclusions which were at variance with the orthodoxies of the Left. Thus in 1949 he wrote that 'There is a line-up of right and left in literature too and for purely literary reasons; but those who are on the left in literature are not always on the left in politics etc; so there is a double game in the relationships between literary avant-gardism and political avant-gardism.' What was being asked of an intellectual was not easy. He had to go through a process of renunciation, carrying out that introspective examination without which it is not possible to be an artist but also attempting to be more objective and – Pasolini felt it had to be said – more Christian in his work, placing it in human history. His historicism would not be faithful to Marxism-Leninism, but would presuppose idealism, Catholicism, anarchism, humanitarianism, life and the will to renewal. The Communist writer must, he concluded, be completely free to do what he wished in literature and at the same time be a loyal comrade in politics. It was not an easy stance to adopt; but in this as in other respects Pasolini was not one to opt for easy solutions.

In the autumn of that same year, 1949, Pasolini was threatened with blackmail by a priest, who through an intermediary, indicated that Pasolini should give up politics if he did not want his teaching career to be ruined. The threat was inspired by Pasolini's homosexuality, which was becoming more and more difficult to hide. In October of the same year 'Pier Paolo Pasolini of Casarsa' was charged by the *carabinieri* with enticing young boys. Pasolini did not deny an erotic experience. The scandal exploded. In October he was expelled from the Communist Party, which in its puritanism could not condone homosexuality in a prominent member. The matter came before the courts. Pasolini was acquitted of corruption of minors but found guilty of obscene acts. This was in 1950. In 1952 an appeal dismissed the case for lack of evidence. But in the meantime in the winter of 1949 Pasolini and his mother – abandoning his father in Casarsa – had fled (the word is his) to Rome 'like in a novel'.

Although there are notes and sketches which go back to the period in which the novel is set, *A Dream of Something* was not published until 1962, after, that is to say, the appearance, scandal and literary success of two novels describing in their own highly expressive jargon the life of young proletarians in the slums on the periphery of Rome, many of whom were the sons of peasant immigrants to the city: *Ragazzi di vita* (1955) and *A Violent Life* (1959). At a time when clerical obscurantism had a grip on Italian society, the first of these was denounced to the courts by the Prime Minister's office as an obscene publication, but after a trial in which literary figures, including the poet Ungaretti, provided statements in support of the work, it was cleared because no crime had been committed. Though he was constantly pursued by the legal authorities for his work in film no such charges were laid against *A Dream of Something*, which is less violent in its language and deals not with the urban proletariat but with the youths whom Pasolini had known and been drawn to in Casarsa, Borgo San Giovanni, and the villages and hamlets that are the scene of much of the book. What the novel shares with its predecessors is an episodic technique – one which was to be repeated in Pasolini's films – and a certain objectivity about the representation of the actions of his characters, a distance, a lack of close-ups, a refusal to psychologize. This does not mean that the novel lacks strength of feeling. It is, in fact, suffused with emotion; which is not surprising given that in Friuli Pasolini lived through so many highly formative experiences in his personal, sexual, literary and political life. This is perceptible not only in his pictures of the young men and their families with their instinctive radicalism and traditional Catholicism – the portrait of the Pope is flanked by one of Stalin in the Communist Party rooms – or of the stoicism with which they, like the young girls who have little choice between the tyranny of patriarchy and the seclusion of the convent, endure their fates, but also in his descriptions of the countryside, of the sky and the light, of the Tagliamento river and the Carnic Alps which dominate the whole: to all these his feelings give extraordinary power and intensity. These qualities derive also from the fact that he was celebrating in retrospect a society and a way of life incorporating moral codes which he saw being destroyed by consumerism and by vast changes in social habits, morals and life-styles. He was to denounce them in his *Lutheran Letters* for corrupting not only the youth of Italy but the whole of capitalist society.

Stuart Hood

PART ONE
1948

Our motto must therefore be: reform of
consciousness not by means of dogmas but
through the analysis of consciousness which is
not clear to itself or presents itself in religious or
political forms. It will then be clear that the
world has for long had a dream of something . . .

K. MARX, from a letter to Ruge from Kreuznach
(September 1843)

I

From early in the morning if it is a fine day, the main road and the paths through the field leading to Casale become full of people going to the Easter Monday fair. Little by little the immense open spaces — they are still a wintery green, at once cold and light, tinged here and there by the pink branch of a peach-tree — are swarming with people, walking along, enjoying themselves, playing, running. The horses, unyoked from the little carts, trot and graze along the ditches, youths in their holiday best astride them. The little boys run about waving their swords of peeled branches among the great bicycle enclosures and the little girls in their bright orange, purple or green blouses play peacefully under the elder-trees, which are just beginning to bud. The platforms for the dancing are still empty and the thousands of paper streamers hung on the wire of the lamps scarcely move in the gentlest of breezes blowing from the sea. To the north the circle of mountains of the Carnic Alps submerges in the bright, veiled white light of the first days of spring.

From Ligugnana, Rosa and San Giovanni, which were their villages, unbeknown to one another, Nini Infant, Milio Bartolus and Eligio Pereisson had set out early in the afternoon for the fair along with their mates.

They had known one another for a long time, in fact, for they had met at many other fairs and all three of them belonged to the pick of the youth from the right bank. Nini arrived at Casale by bicycle with his mate from Ligugnana. On his handlebars he had set a branch of hawthorn and since he had been a little drunk since morning he passed no girl whom he did not assail with wild and gallant cries. He was in high spirits. The moment he arrived in Casale he threw his bicycle into the enclosure with the gesture of someone who feels he is one of the leading personages of the festival even though he is a stranger, and the boys who looked after the bicycles immediately treated him with a kindness which was at once attentive, mocking and slightly ironical. Having left the bicycle in their hands and carrying only a sprig of almond, which he stuck between his teeth, he set off at once to take possession of the scene.

Meanwhile there arrived from Rosa a company of boys — no less boisterous than he — of between fifteen and twenty years of age with their jackets on their shoulders and jerseys with big coloured stripes on their chests. Among them was Milo with blond, slightly wavy hair and eyes that looked like blue crystal, with his accordion slung round his neck and no sooner — just like Nini — had his group got rid of their bicycles than he furiously struck up a *paso doble* to the laughter and cries of his companions.

Then the third, Eligio Pereisson, arrived standing in a cart full of girls and small boys. He was driving a white horse, which shook its head and slid about among the crowd. Meanwhile the girls were singing and waving handkerchiefs and almond-tree twigs which they had torn off on the way. The moment they reached the open space for the fair, the girls swarmed off and Eligio remained behind to see to the horse, helped by his brother, Onorino. When everything was in order he turned round to look for his mates who had vanished amidst the confusion.

Nini, Eligio, Milio were all at the age when an accordion is a thing of importance. It was thus that they got to know one another — through Milio's harmonium, which he was playing among his mates under two hawthorn bushes and Nini was there already with his hands in his pockets, standing and listening to him. He had a slightly ironical and provocative air and seemed about to say something — perhaps it was a criticism of the *paso doble* or a remark or perhaps a compliment. At all events he had a way of looking that was very assured and merry, but the other boys from Rosa had hardly noticed him — not so Milio, however, who had glanced at him quickly and was now playing with particular dash, putting everything he had into it, almost as if he were playing for him.

Meanwhile the other boy had come up and had placed himself at Nini's side. They looked at each other stealthily but did not have the courage to strike up a conversation. Suddenly, however, the boys from Rosa decided to move off – perhaps to the platforms for the dancing (which had not yet begun) or to the innkeeper's booth – and dragged with them Milio, who continued to play. Left alone by the hawthorn bushes in this way, Nini and Eligio glanced at each other and it was Nini who made up his mind: 'You are from San Giovanni, aren't you?' he asked formally.

'Yes,' replied the other. 'And if I'm not mistaken you are from Ligugnana. We've often seen each other at fairs.'

'On Sunday I met you at Mure with a pretty girl – I know her, she's from Gruaro – and she had a friend who was pretty too whom I've never managed to talk to.'

'They'll maybe come here today,' said Eligio, 'if you like I can introduce you.'

'Marvellous! Shall we go and drink a glass?'

'Let's go,' said Eligio happily.

By now their friendship was established. The two youths had been wanting to get to know each other for so long and had been looking at each other. Once there had almost been a quarrel between them because of an accidental push they had given each other when dancing. And it was from that moment that they loved each other. Now, after the first words, a kind of enthusiasm, of warmth, began to come into their talk that made everything beautiful: the idea of going to drink a glass, which was the most commonplace one they could have at that moment, felt amazing to them; and, especially after they had drunk not one but two or three glasses of wine, they hung on each other's lips as if certain things – the organization of a fair, the skill of a little orchestra or the high spirits of the girls from Gruaro – seemed themes that were being discussed for the first time since the creation of the world. Nini was frivolous, Eligio crazy, but at that moment both had an air that was very severe, almost proud. They laughed as if they were laughing between themselves for very special reasons, which the rest of the young people around them had to listen to in wonder.

The two sisters from Gruaro arrived half an hour later and the boys, catching sight of them, ran at once to accost them. Eligio laughed with his blond boy's face which was just tinged with pink and with the blue blades of his transparent eyes, but when he got close to the girls he suddenly became serious and after greeting them with the assurance of an old friend, said: 'I want you to meet a mate of mine.'

Nini stood a little to one side with his capricious and brilliant smile. Eligio put a hand on his shoulder and said his name: 'Nini' and then Nini drew close, politely held out his hand and repeated with an embarrassment hidden by his lively cheekiness: 'Giovanni Infant — I am very pleased to meet you.' And they, being pleased too, said their names in their turn very formally. They were pretty and well got up with their chestnut hair and the permanent wave that had been the fashion two or three years earlier; well built, too, including their shoulders, with beautiful breasts under their light dresses, one turquoise and the other maroon. They had worn them for the first time the day before, which was Easter, and they were still as immaculate as they had been on the dressmaker's table. In fact, they themselves were the dressmakers and indeed their hands didn't look red and in their bearing they had something which set them off from the peasant girls. That was precisely what took the fancy of Nini and Eligio. They at once assumed an air of protectiveness and easy confidence. They too wanted to be better than the peasant boys. In fact Nini was wearing a cowboy shirt and Eligio an American one of the same sky-blue as his eyes.

The little orchestra had begun to play. The music spread gaily all round and was lost in the meadows. That was all the two couples were waiting for and they began to dance from the first number. They were alone on the platform along with another couple of young men — perhaps two people from the fair — and the eyes of the young boys and the youths who had come running up round the platform were turned on them. They were two good dancers of the kind that give life to an occasion. From the third or fourth number they gave immediate proof of their skill and on the half-empty platform, with the excuse that they were taking advantage of the free space, they danced a boogie-woogie which enchanted the callow spectators and slightly shocked — although it made them laugh — the old mothers who were keeping an eye on the girls. Nini and Eligio wished to excel themselves so as to be able to admire each other. When the number was over they sought each other out among the other couples and went under the booth housing the orchestra to chat, talking about certain new dance-steps which they alone knew. They were on good terms with the members of the orchestra and could ask for the songs they wanted. The violinist, who was the leader, a dark and scatter-brained youth from Rosa, knew both of them and every so often leaned over to make some joke — a new source of admiration of the two strangers by their young peers and the smaller boys.

Milio appeared on the platform for only half an hour along with an unknown girl. He was not a great dancer like Nini and Eligio and was somewhat overshadowed. Then after exchanging several glances with the two unknown friends he went off.

They caught up with him again after supper. The two sisters from Gruaro had left. There was a lack of girls; those who had come from San Giovanni with Eligio did not know how to dance. They kept together in a bunch along with the smaller brothers of Eligio, Onorino and Livio, and on the platform there was a great crush. Nini and Eligio went up and down in the crowd along with their mates, who had introduced themselves. They danced little and preferred to be cheeky to the girls from Codroipo. It was in this way that they bumped into the crowd from Rosa. It was a very gay company all set for great things. They were like incendiaries looking for something to burn, to make a huge bonfire of it to show the boys from Casale or Codroipo the mettle of the boys from the other bank of the Tagliamento river. They had not found anything to burn, but to judge from the brightness of their eyes it was just as if they had. Nini and Eligio, when they caught sight of Milio with his group, shouted 'Hey, boys' and the others replied 'Hey'.

So the other friendship of the day was made.

Milio seized the accordion and struck up a *Te Deum* to a march rhythm. Now things were getting going. They went to the inn and baptized their friendship. Rapid, gay confidences were made with the warmth that made everything fine and new. Then gradually, as the atmosphere became more heated, they got round to the jokes. This was still the quiet phase of their talk.

Eligio was wonderful at telling jokes. As they listened to him everyone laughed in an excited way, finishing up every time with the same, regular guffaw. All the most daring subjects were reviewed. It was a kind of examination which the three friends passed with honours. Then came the time for singing. It was an infernal chorus – the boys from Rosa, who had been drunk for a while now, like damned souls, sang one song after another, the dirtiest ones they knew. When the repertory seemed to be exhausted, there was always someone who struck up a song more daring than the last – if that were possible. Nini, inflamed by the wine and as light as a bird, kept the Mysteries in reserve. And when the boys from Rosa had been drained dry he struck up. At once the choir took up after him solemnly bellowing over the empty bottles and the overturned glasses.

It was already late at night – it must have been at least half-past one. The meadows were already almost empty, the dancing was over and the people from the fair were unscrewing the lamps from the trestle-tables. But the booth that served as an inn would still be open for a while. It was the crowd from the other bank of the Tagliamento that kept their spirits up and turned the booth into a fairground. The youths from Rosa continued to sing loud enough to burst their lungs with their feet on the table, laughing and looking into one another's eyes and every so often taking another sip of wine. Nini was sitting on the knees of Basilio, his mate from Ligugnano, and sang with his laughing eyes standing out of his head and his coal-black hair shining with sweat and brilliantine. For all of them it was very important to know a song and each one sought to impose his own songs one after another but joined in those of his comrades with passionate abandon.

Eligio Pereisson had a gift for song. He was seated on the table among the glasses of red wine and held a broom in his hands as if it were a guitar. At a certain moment he began to sing, but what on earth was he singing? All of them listened to him in a state of surprise without understanding a word.

It was a boogie rhythm that he sang – just like a Negro: *tving, ca ubang, bredar, lov, aucester, tving, tving, morou thear*. He sat huddled over the broom with one leg thrown over the other. He looked into the eyes of his listeners and laughed, did not cease laughing for a moment with those burning eyes of his that seemed like two pieces of glass. It was impossible to understand what he was singing – whether it was a joke or some crazy idea – but at all events it never ended and he kept on laughing, beating out a perfect rhythm on the broom and finding, from goodness knows where, words and tune: *den bredar tuinding fear.* Then suddenly he stopped with a great laugh, throwing away the broom. The others also laughed like mad and took up the chorus, but Eligio, huddled in his chair, after a little went on singing to himself his mysterious song.

Then suddenly Nini awoke from his dazed state, rose to his feet and cried desperately: 'Down with women – those whores' and fell back on to Basilio's knees swallowing a glass of wine. The others shouted like him: 'Down with women, long live cunts.' And they struck up a song they had learned from the soldiers at Casarsa: 'I have a pistol loaded with little golden bullets.'

At this song Nini half reopened his eyes and staring in front of him with his glass in his hand gave assent: 'Yes, fucking Madonna.' He seemed extraordinarily happy to give his approval, then his eyes turned to his raised hand with the glass in it, rested on it in curiosity and a moment later the glass, thrown with all his force, smashed against the wall of the booth. 'I am happy, God damn it,' he added. Eligio slowly took up a glass and sent it to keep the other company with a sharp bang.

The owner of the inn came grumbling up to say that glasses were expensive and they should stop. The other youths who crowded the booth turned towards the outsiders' table with an air that did not say much but was for this very reason not without a note of threat. Nini felt greatly offended and made some remarks, half polite and half annoyed, which were merely the lead-up to much stormier statements. The owner rebuked him, still in a subdued tone, but he too was already somewhat nervous. Then Nini flew into a rage at the whole village with its 'boorish peasants'. But the owner went off. The boys from Rosa began to sing again to smooth over the row; Nini would not go along with them and continued to hurl insults at the local people. Then suddenly he gave over. He and Milio looked at each other with affection; but Milio was a little less drunk and still talked a certain amount of sense. So when from one moment to the next

9

Nini shouted to the company that he needed to piss and that he was going to piss under the table, Milio laughed and tried to stop him. But it was no use. Nini brought his chair up to the table and kept his word. The others round about him sang with renewed enthusiasm.

From Casale to San Giovanni was about ten kilometres by road. They went to the bicycle park where their bicycles were the only ones remaining and a very sleepy boy was waiting for them. The moment he saw Nini he began to smile secretly, maliciously, and Nini, who was drunk, looked him over from head to foot. The boy to make things easier offered him a glass of wine, for even the beardless guards had taken part in the wild gaiety of the evening and half a bottle of wine was left over. 'Give it here,' shouted Nini, 'Jees — ' He seized the neck of the bottle and drank, then let the bottle fall to the ground and while the others were taking care of the bicycles, finished the bout of peeing he had begun in the booth, singing the while. 'Gosh!' said the boy from the bicycle park and to show his amazement and amusement he doubled up laughing so that he almost touched the ground. Eligio had been abandoned by his gang from San Giovanni, who had left some hours earlier with the cart driven by his small brothers. So he had to be taken on someone's cross-bar. But he didn't want anyone else to have such hard work and wished to pedal himself. So there was a long argument between him and Milio. At last Eligio brought it to an end by saying that while he gave him a ride Milio could play the accordion. Then Milio sat on the handlebars, leant his head on the shoulder of his new mate and began to play. And the company set off for the other bank of the Tagliamento amid the cries of the boy from the bicycle park and of the people from the fair.

But the bicycle-ride and the cold night air instead of putting some sense into their heads merely made them more drunk. 'These whores of bicycles,' Nini shouted seeing that his bicycle constantly veered towards the edge of the road without, however, ever going over it. Under the moonlight, which sparkled in the pastures, they rode along shouting like demons just a little sad that perhaps there was no one to hear them. In fact, the road which ran from San Daniele to join the main road from Venice to Udine a little below Codroipo is the most deserted in the whole of

Friuli. To the left, under the moon, stretched the magazines of the powder-factory which once upon a time used to blow up every so often, breaking the windows in all the neighbouring villages. And the boys from Rosa, skirting it, seemed to wish to recall and to drown its ancient explosions. Then under the immense beam of blue and dusty moonlight there appeared, stretching boundlessly from the mountains to the plain, the shingle-bed of the Tagliamento. At full speed the boys rode on to the great long bridge but after barely a hundred metres one of them from Rosa braked suddenly, threw his bicycle at full length on the asphalt as if it were a toy shouting: 'Wait boys, I have to have a piss.' Everyone braked and kept him company, lining up all along the parapet. Nini too took his place along with them but after a moment asked himself at the top of his lungs: 'What am I doing here with my thing in my hand? I don't need any more.' Then he lifted his bicycle from the ground as if it were a feather and went off along the long causeway singing. The others laughed in a row along the bridge. 'Let's give the Tagliamento some water,' shouted Milio, 'it never has any.'

At the first houses in Casarsa they began to sing once more at the top of their voices. They wanted to wake up the whole village. And when they were in the square, Milio, still leaning on Eligio and sitting on the handlebar, quietened them all for a moment with a shout and on his accordion struck up 'The Red Flag'.

And they all followed him shouting.

Milio and Nini did not go home with the others but stopped at San Giovanni at Eligio's for a while.

They entered Eligio's house as if it were that of an old friend. While he went to get the wine and some cheese, they began to examine the photographs stuck in the glass of the sideboard, looking at the women cousins and their friends, dressed in their best, and looking like statues. In the little kitchen with its red-tiled floor, smoked beams in the ceiling and whitewashed walls, the deep silence of the last hours of the night reigned. From the rooms above they could hear the breathing of the sleepers while from the pig-sty every so often came the grunting of the sow as she dreamed. Eligio appeared with the wine bottle and a bit of cheese. 'We'll have to eat polenta,' he whispered, 'the

11

bread is finished.' They sat under the chimney-piece with their feet on the stone and ate and talked. They weren't very sure what they said — they were talking to each other. And that gave them immense satisfaction. When the flask was finished Milio and Nini took leave of Eligio. He accompanied them to the door of the courtyard. 'Goodbye, Eligio!' shouted Nini, 'goodbye, keep well.' But when he had taken a few steps he turned back. 'No — I want to give you a kiss,' he said. 'Come here!' Eligio laughed and offered his cheek.

'No, on the mouth, damn it,' said Nini, 'we must kiss on the mouth.' They kissed, mimicking two lovers.

'Goodbye, Eligio,' the two of them shouted as they rode off on their bicycles.

'Goodbye, goodbye,' shouted Eligio from the doorway standing on the deserted street where the moon beat down.

'Goodbye, Eligio,' called Nini once again, turning round.

II

At the workers' club the air was burning. The last groups of young and old drunks were sitting round disordered tables, wet with spilt wine. Through the open windows the spring air entered in waves, fresh and dark. Everyone was shouting and yelling, dazed by the wine. Nini, Eligio and Milio were round a little table along with a group of boys from San Giovanni and had begun the finale to their Sunday; but their gaiety was a little forced. Each one had a lot of thoughts in his heart and little money in his pocket. Then Eligio began to tell jokes and they gathered round his voice which by its mere tone made you want to laugh, reserving for the final moment their ponderous guffaw. Then they began to sing but two or three went off when things were at a pitch because it was late by now and next day, at dawn, the byre awaited them. Eligio's young brothers too, Onorino and Livo, with their friends, Chini and Ivano, left saying good-night timidly because they still had short trousers. The others stayed on; they seemed unable to rid themselves of the thought that they had only fifty lire left in their pockets and that the other two hundred had flown away like smoke during the fair. Nini seemed to be singing his Mysteries to himself with his dark head leaning on the wall and his knees up against the table. At a certain moment an old man came up, glass in hand.

'How are the young folk?' he shouted at the boys and staggered.

'Fine – and you?' said Milo.

'Me – I'm old,' he said and winked.

13

'Long live cunt,' said Nini with his eyes shut. The old man bent over him and began to tell him in his ear, but with a loud voice so that everyone could hear, a story about women that had happened to him when he was an immigrant in Germany before the other war. It was an inconclusive story and when he had finished Nini opened his eyes and said: 'You're drunk — go to bed.'

'Drunk? Me?' said the old man with a solemn and indignant air, bending his knees with a ridiculous gesture like a barrister in full flight. 'When I began to drink my two bottles a day you weren't even in your mother's belly! Remember that!'

'I'll remember,' said Nini shrugging and shutting his eyes again he began to sing once more: 'And I who am little . . . '

The old man turned towards the whole company: 'I had travelled all over all the Americas and all the Germanies when I was your age!' he shouted with a laughing, swollen face as red as fire.

'And what did you get out of it?' Eligio asked him with an ironical air but a familiar tone. Everyone, expecting him to tell some tall story, got ready to laugh.

'A kick up the arse,' replied the old man and went back to his friends near the bar but a little later he very quietly approached again. 'You young people,' he began to shout, 'are soft. What are you doing here in Italy! Italy! Get away with you! You can travel all over the world but you'll never come across shit like in Italy. An Italian is a thief. If he can do you he'll do you in every possible way. And the poor are worse than the rich. He only needs a couple of coins in his pocket to forget his comrades and begin to behave like a shit himself. Get away, you young people, go abroad! Do like me, boys, who've travelled all over the world, the Americas, Belgium, Germany. Get away, boys, from this bloody Italy. Do like me who've come back poorer than before and with lice.'

Everyone laughed. The old man did a pirouette as if to go back again to the group of older men — Pieri Susanna, the secretary of the Party, Blasut and the others who were chatting at the bar. But when he had already half turned round his eyes focused on the group of boys and, staring at them seriously, he said with an astute and confidential air: 'Look at the other day —

Domenico's son – the fair-haired one – what's he called?'

'Rico,' said Eligio.

'Yes, Rico, that's right,' exclaimed the old man. 'He was supposed to go to Argentina and he'd booked a place on the ship leaving in August of last year. But two or three days before leaving he gets a letter where it says that his place on the boat had been given to someone going on government business. And d'you know what had happened? You with the dark hair – '

'Me?' said Nini. 'What am I supposed to know about it? Let them get on with it.'

'Forget about the government. Somebody had taken the place who had ten or twelve thousand lire to hand over to the man at the agency. That's your Italian for you.'

'And you wouldn't have done the same?' said Eligio laughing.

'The other day,' the old man went on, 'Rico gets a new letter that says, damn it, that this time too the place has been taken by someone from the government. He was supposed to leave in March and he's still at home. He'd asked the bank for a loan of two hundred thousand lire for the journey – he's been at home for a year without work and he's used up almost all of it. Luckily he had a friend in Genoa who told him that for ten or twelve thousand lire he could pass himself off as someone from the government too!

'So,' the old man went on from the doorway that led into the little bar, 'some poor chap in some other village in Italy will see a letter arrive saying that his place has been reserved for someone from the government. And this man from the government is Domenico's Rico.'

For the third time he turned back to the old men, skipping. But no sooner was he in the other room than he turned threateningly towards the boys and whispered: 'Kill them all!' and ran his hand over his neck like a knife.

'Kill them all!' he repeated with a shout and turned back to his group after another wink to the young people.

At that moment Jacu came in; he was drunk and had heard the old man's last words.

'Kill them all, damn it,' he said too and let himself fall into a chair near Eligio.

'How are things, cousin?' said the latter.

15

'The way they are when you don't have a single coin in your pocket,' he said and drew a wallet from the inside pocket of his jacket, opened it carefully and showed that, apart from a couple of photographs and his identity card, it was empty.

'Cheer up, comrade!' cried Nino, 'courage!' He got up, poured a glass of wine and said to him: 'Drink up and tell them to go to hell.'

Jacu emptied the glass in a gulp, put back his wallet and repeated: 'Kill them all!'

'Keep your chin up,' said Eligio cheerfully, 'the time will come when we'll make them all pay for it. But meantime there's no point getting upset like that.'

The old man had come back again, with his hat on, staggering; he laughed and stared at Jacu maliciously. He stood like that for a moment, then leant over him and murmured with a grimace: 'Tighten your belt!'

'Drop dead,' said Jacu, so drunk that he was pale and the skin of his face almost green. 'The good old days are over,' shouted the old man with a grin, 'when you used to go and work for the Germans!'

'Why, didn't you and your son go too?' said Jacu contemptuously. 'Everybody went.'

'And he,' said Eligio, 'didn't give a damn for the bombing. It was great, wasn't it?'

But the old man paid no attention. Rubbing finger and thumb together he turned to the company and shouted: 'Money! Money! How many trains did you rob at Carsara, you people from San Giovanni? Eh? Why? Were the Germans shooting at the stars?' And he made a triumphant pirouette.

'Were we supposed to let them take it all back to Germany?' said Milio smugly.

'Forget about this old fool,' said Nini.

'Tell me, you with the dark hair,' said the old man calmly without ever ceasing to grin, 'where did the money come from that you had a good time with last year?'

'I earned it.'

'And what did you do?' asked the old man seriously.

Nini began to laugh. 'I was cook at the English headquarters at Carsara,' he said.

'Now the bonanza's over, the bonanza's over,' shouted the old man. 'The English have gone back to England and the camps are shut.'

'Thank God for that,' said Eligio. 'That way your son isn't in danger any more of being taken and shot for stealing blankets.'

'You,' said the old man, stabbing with his finger, 'didn't you work there too?'

'Yes,' said Eligio.

'And you had a good time?'

'I could do with it for the rest of my life!'

The old man looked at him for a moment, blinking his eyes; then he undid his trouser belt and tightened it by three or four holes. And he began to laugh loudly.

'Go on, go to bed,' said Milio.

'Where are you from?' asked the old man.

'I'm from Rosa,' said Milio challengingly.

'And what do you do?'

'I'm a peasant – always have been and always will be.'

'And now there are no more ration cards,' proclaimed the old man, 'and the women don't come up any more from Trieste. You didn't half pinch flour from the landlords, you peasants.'

'That's nonsense,' said Milio.

The old man thrust his hat deep down over his eyes, ran towards the door to the street laughing like mad; then at the door he stopped, became suddenly serious, and stretching out his arms towards the boys repeated in a low voice: 'Kill them all!'

Then he went off along the street singing. Nini rose to his feet and struck up the group's old song: 'I have a pistol loaded with little golden balls.'

It was a year now since Nini, Eligio and Milo had got to know one another and they had been through a lot together since that Easter Monday when they had been very formal to begin with. Besides the party to celebrate the conscript class of 1929, there had been the fairs in all the villages round about – at Cintello, Savorgnano, Gleris, and then that great one at San Pietro e Paolo, at Valvasone, and at Saletto, Teglio, Cordovado. It had been great at Cordovado. After dancing and drinking all night, at about two in the morning they had decided to go and have a bathe. They arrived shouting and singing at the lake which shone so smoothly under the stars. They undressed quickly in the bushes and threw themselves naked into the water. It had just stopped raining and the grass was wet and the branches of the acacias dripped; everything gleamed in the moon. The boys from Rosa ran about naked among the trees to warm themselves. Nini, putting on his pants in the beam of moonlight, was telling the others about the girl from Ramuscello whom he had taken home and Eligio, who did not believe him, was sending him up.

Now the Easter festivities had come round again. 'Tomorrow,' shouted Eligio in the club, which by now was half-empty, 'we're going to Casale.'

'That will be fun,' cried Nini happily.

'But these will be the last fair booths, comrades,' said Milio. 'Here it's a case of die of hunger or get out!'

'Have your papers come?' asked Eligio.

'Not yet, but I should get them in a day or two.'

'Maybe I'll go away too,' said Nini, looking round.

'Where to?' said Pieri Susanna who had come up. He was scratching his head under his cap in surprise because it was the first time Nini had mentioned emigrating and he said it with such careless arrogance that it was impossible to take him seriously.

'To Yugoslavia,' answered Nini in all simplicity. 'There at least there's Communism!'

'By yourself?'

'No, there are five or six of us in Ligugnana who have this idea. And then there's someone here,' and he winked at Eligio. 'But nothing's settled yet — we'll see.' And he drank the little wine that was left in the bottle.

'Hey, comrade,' Jacu shouted at him. 'Leave me a drop.' There was still a little and Jacu sucked it out of the neck of the bottle. By now they were the last customers at the club. The others had left but were still talking in the street in the fresh, sonorous silence of the Easter night.

III

On the 14th of July 1948, Nini and Eligio, along with Antonio and Pietro Nonis, Basilio Nio and Germano Giacomuzzi, left Ligugnana to go to Yugoslavia.

All their mates came to see them to the station at Carsara and drink a last glass of white wine together. Milio had brought his accordion and they said goodbye singing and shouting.

And weeping too. But these were days of hope, the war seemed a long way off now and for the young people life was beginning.

At about four in the afternoon they arrived in Gorizia and to pass the time had the idea of climbing up to the castle. From up there on top of the fortifications, which rose on a hill-top, one could see, running along a green and blue expanse of hills and mountains, the frontier of Yugoslavia and Yugoslavia itself seemingly asleep in the sun.

With their bundles at their feet, the boys looked in silence towards that limpid horizon, which was deep-blue and drenched in a light that took one's breath away, and ran along the curves of the foothills among woods, villages and clearings. Right under the castle on the side of a hill one could see, not more than two or three hundred metres away, a white road which traced its way through houses and gardens. Men were walking along it. A woman came to a window to shake a cloth. There it was no longer Italy. It felt as if the world had come to an end or that an entirely new world was beginning, free and bright.

The next day, early in the morning, they reached Cividale.

Leaving their things in an inn they went round the town

looking for the man whom Germano's brother had talked about in Gorizia. Instead of the man they found the *carabinieri*. And it was lucky that they were going about without luggage. They spent a good part of the morning and of the afternoon in the barracks and when they were let out at about five they immediately resumed their search. But where could they find this man? The light was beginning to go and they were hungry. They made for the countryside at a venture and crossed the Ponte del Diavolo over the Natisone, which gleamed under the cloudy sky. There they turned down a small road along the river which made its way through terraced meadows, between little stone walls and clumps of briars and elders. They sat down in an open spot and began to eat the bread and salami they had in their pockets. No one said anything. They did not say so but they were tired and discouraged. Where could they find a man who could act as guide? And, meantime, where could they go to sleep? Nini as usual seemed to make a game of it all, shrugged and said, 'Damn it, comrades, we'll find a way.'

In the end, at the inn where they had left their baggage, they found a man, sitting half-drunk over a litre of red wine, who after chatting a little offered to guide them over the frontier.

By now it was eleven o'clock at night. He took them out into the courtyard and said they should go ahead and wait for him in a little place beyond the town at the foot of the mountains. It was raining. They waited for a good while in the rain on the crest of the hill among the trees. At last, when they had given up hope, the man arrived from further down the mountain.

'It is six or seven hours' walk,' he said. They began to walk with their heavy bundles. The man was drunk.

They walked like this all night and their march was very difficult because they couldn't see more than two steps ahead. The path was full of stones and the branches of the trees struck them in the face. It was raining hard.

The path ran all the time through the wood. Only occasionally did it pass through a clearing on a steep slope. Then the thick darkness would lift a little and they could look down into the emptiness of a valley or along the flanks of the mountains, which were black with woods. Often they had to leave the road and push through where the trees were thick, along paths that could hardly be distinguished. Towards dawn the Slovene said: 'Here you are boys, this is the frontier.' He asked for six thousand lire for his work and turned back.

They began to walk again towards the spot he had pointed out to them but they found nothing. They walked for another quarter of an hour and there was no sign of the frontier. It was morning by now and it was still raining. Soaked through and dead with fatigue, they ate a piece of bread sitting on the rocks. After a little they set off again. 'We'll be in Yugoslavia now,' said Nini. 'We'll have crossed the frontier.' But nothing had changed around them – always the same woods and every so often the valleys and mountains, which came into sight in glimpses which were always the same, lost in silence and solitude.

Nini, who little by little had convinced himself that they had crossed the frontier, showed no more signs of being tired and walked along happily and lightly, shouting to the other boys from time to time: 'Cheer up, comrades, we are in Yugoslavia!'

But Germano, who was walking at the head of the group, tall and thin with his great partisan's head of hair, still seemed uncertain and Nini made fun of him. He was excited and almost began to sing. The others, too, felt almost at ease and had taken out a cigarette to pass round. Suddenly – they were walking along a valley and by now it was almost day – they saw two or three hundred metres away the Italian flag and under it a sentry. It took their breath away. This time it was no joke. They threw themselves on the ground among the bushes and stayed there for a while without moving.

'What shall we do?' said Nini.

'Talk more quietly to begin with,' muttered Bazilio angrily.

'Stop!' said Germano to the two Nonis who were trying to get a closer look at the post where the flag was flying.

Luckily it had stopped raining half an hour before and the July sun was clearing the sky. They stayed there for a while without knowing what to do. At last Nini made up his mind.

'I'm going on,' he said. 'I'm not going back to Italy.'

'Off we go,' whispered Germano.

They crept through the bushes and trees of the wood, which was fairly thick, and clambered up the slope. When they were well out of sight of the sentry they began to run, crouching and trying to keep always in the cover of the branches. It was thus that without knowing it they passed the line of white frontier posts.

They walked on quickly for another twenty minutes or so, then in the midst of a clearing they found a man – perhaps a forester – and asked him if they were in Italy or Yugoslavia.

He looked at them without saying anything and after a little went off into the undergrowth. He had gone to call the Slavs. The boys sat down on the grass. Eligio stretched himself out although it was wet and in a minute had fallen asleep. The others smoked in silence. They did not say so but they were worried and thinking of home, of Ligugnana and San Giovanni, which were now so far off and in another time, and of their mates back there who at this moment, with the first sunlight and just out of bed, were chatting in the school playground.

In less than a quarter of an hour the forester appeared with a Slav soldier armed with a tommy-gun. They were taken from the spot to the command post about a kilometre away where they were interrogated. 'Why did you leave clandestinely?' asked an officer. 'To work in Yugoslavia,' the boys, who had the Communist badge in their button-holes and were proud of it, replied promptly. They had no doubt, in fact, that the Yugoslavs would see to it that they could sleep and eat. Instead the order came to leave and, led by two armed soldiers, they had to do eighteen kilometres, soaked and unfed as they were.

They walked as if in a dream without understanding anything any more. Before their eyes passed woods, roads, unknown villages, which were almost deserted.

First Germano and then Nini fell to the ground exhausted. The others helped to lift them up and then to walk, almost weeping. 'Cheer up, comrades,' they kept saying, 'we'll soon be there.'

Nini walked along cursing. They reached Tolmino when it was night. There they had to go round the village for more than an hour looking for somewhere to sleep. But they found nowhere so they were taken to the jail. It was already late. They slept on the ground, some in the kitchen, some in the corridors. In the morning they were given a little coffee and made to leave again, this time without an escort, with orders to go to Santa Lucia di Tolmino.

When they reached Santa Lucia, after a walk of fifteen kilometres, they were told to move on again, this time by train, and arrived at Verpoile.

The place seemed to be uninhabited. It was scattered along the bottom of a little valley. The sun struck the white walls of the little houses and of the gardens and there was no sign of life around, on the black and green flanks of the hills, apart from an occasional noise from the deserted station at the other end of the village. They went towards the centre of the village, a big square on a slope, and it too was deserted. In the house – it was peeling and riddled by machine-gun bullets – which had once been the *carabinieri* post, they found a Yugoslav guard, who, cursing and sweating, took them a little way out of the village, to a big, bare building like a factory: it was the house for illegal immigrants. In the evening they were not given anything to eat and they were forced to sleep on the floor or on camp-beds without mattresses. The next day they were given something to eat only at midday and in the evening nothing but a little bread. They were dejected. Nini and the others at home during festival nights sometimes devoured up to four loaves with mortadella in the morning after the dancing. Now at Verpoile they were dying of hunger. They got into the habit – just as they were without having eaten – of walking up and down the village, of not doing anything, or of lying stretched out for hours with their legs apart at the side of the road or on the pavements. Sometimes they played cards; but no one really felt like it because their bellies were empty. One day they were taking a walk beyond the village, silent and depressed. Eligio and Nini had a different curse for each step and the others laughed to hear them. Then a peasant came from the village and approached them. He was a Slav but he spoke Italian well.

'Which of you would like to work for me in the fields?' he asked.

'What will you give us?' asked Germano in turn. He was tough with his hands in his pockets and a scowling face. He wanted to strike a good bargain.

'Twenty dinars,' said the peasant, 'and food.'

'Me!' shouted Nini; the others had been too slow and Nini followed the man, hoping finally to get a good meal.

It was a marvellous morning. The hills were full of shadows but their round backs were bright green in the sun and the valley was full of light. Nini and the man first went home to get the scythes and the rakes, then with their gear on their shoulders they set out. Nini felt cheerful. It was a very long time since he had used a scythe and although it was a peasant's hardest work he felt a kind of nostalgia for it.

The meadow where they were to work, however, never appeared although they walked for almost an hour. At last six or seven kilometres further on there it was — immense, among the woods, full of thick green weeds. There was not much to cut, not more than an hour's work; then they went a little further down to rake the hay. Meantime midday had come; the bell of a distant village could just be heard echoing with its weak and festive peal behind the hill. The meadows were immense and unending. Nini was so hungry that he was seeing double, but he made a great effort to rake vigorously to show the peasant how good the Italian boys were. One o'clock came, then two, then three and of lunch there was not the least sign. At last a woman arrived on a cart with a basket. The two men threw down their rakes and ran towards her at the edge of the wood. The meal consisted of soup with a couple of potatoes.

Nini, who was almost crying, swallowed down the two spoonfuls of soup and the two potatoes in less than a minute and with such haste that the peasant looked at him and smiled, saying: 'Eat, eat, boy, because young people are hungry.'

Then they set to work again; there were still two steep fields and then the hay had to be loaded on to the cart. When at about half-past six the cart was loaded, the swampy ground gave way, the wheels sank into it and the frightened horses broke the shaft. So they had to leave all the hay there because it was too late to reload it and they went back home. When they arrived it was already dark with the peasant cursing in Italian, but coldly and resignedly, not like at home. Nini who was not worried about the hay could think only of supper. That drop of soup had merely moistened his empty stomach, but he hoped the supper would be better, thinking that this was their way here. Meantime he was dying of hunger. But supper was like lunch: a bowl of polenta and milk. So Nini returned to his waiting comrades with twenty dinars in his pocket and while he went to bed with his stomach easier than other evenings Eligio made fun of him: 'Eat, boy, eat!'

But the next day they began to work for the Yugoslavs: there was the school at Verpoile, which the Germans had blown up, to rebuild. They worked for a fortnight for nothing and with hardly anything to eat. On July 2nd they were summoned to Headquarters where they were told to write a diary of their lives from 1943 to 1947. Next day Nini, Eligio, Germano and Basilio were given permission to leave. Accompanied by a Yugoslav policeman, first in a bus and then in a train, they arrived at Fiume.

IV

The sea, on the night they arrived at Fiume and wandered about
for more than three hours – dead with hunger and fatigue,
looking for the torpedo factory where they were to work – seemed
to be a huge expanse of pitch, cold, gloomy in the light of the
lamps that cast a reddish light along the Dalmatian coast. It was
frightening, and very different from the sea at Caorle – the one
they had seen for the first time in their lives, just after the war,
when they had gone on a trip with the 'Garibaldi Pioneers' and
with Pieri Susanna at their head, still full of hope, shouting:
'Keep it up, boys, because we're making the revolution!' A
beautiful sea, all calm and blue, where parties of peasants were
eating breakfast and covering the little beach with yellow paper
and empty bottles. And Milio playing his accordion. And Eligio
singing like mad. And Nini scratching his stomach.

After they had been in Fiume for a couple of weeks, however,
and had been taken on at the torpedo factory, things began to get
a bit better. Nini and the other comrades began to get used to the
city and the sea. Until three in the afternoon they worked in the
factory, then they were free. One day, to pass the rest of the
afternoon a little more cheerfully Basilio had the idea of going to
the beach. 'Goodness knows how much it will cost!' said
Germano.

'Don't you remember at Caorle?' said Nini. 'Those who wanted
paid the bathing establishment for a cabin and those who didn't
undressed on the open beach.'

So they set off along the beach looking for a place where

bathing was free. Now they felt the sea to be exactly as it had been at Caorle, except that in the distance the mountains of Dalmatia and of the islands could be clearly seen; and it was always calm under a blazing sun. They walked a good way along the front and at last found a place where the beach narrowed, became wild, almost black and full of rocks. There were a lot of young people from Fiume, Slovenes and Italians, who had installed themselves there, deafening air and sea with their shouts. 'Shall we sit here?' asked Eligio. 'There's too much din.' said Germano. 'Let's go a bit further on.' 'I'm stopping here,' said Nini.

He jumped down on to the sand among the bushes and in less than a minute was in his pants. While the others undressed he struck up a conversation with a boy from Fiume. 'How much do you pay to go to a bathing-station?' he asked him. The boy mentioned a sum in dinars and Nini, having made a calculation, found it was about fifty lire. He went to tell Germano. 'Tomorrow we'll go to the bathing-station,' he concluded happily.

The boy from Fiume approached them. 'Where are you from?' he asked.

'We're from Friuli,' said Nini proudly. 'In Italy,' he added, 'we couldn't go on living with that bloody government. Long live Tito, for God's sake!' The boy from Fiume laughed and said nothing. 'Tell us,' Nini went on, 'are there pretty young ladies at the bathing-stations?' 'There's some marvellous cunt,' said the other. 'Ah, boys,' shouted Nini to his mates, 'I feel like having fun. Tomorrow who doesn't want to come along and get to know these pretty girls from Fiume?'

Next day they went to the bathing-station. There were indeed pretty girls from Fiume — in fact they were beautiful — girls the like of which Nini had never seen, blonde, with long, smooth hair falling over their shoulders, or gathered up under rubber bathing-caps, with such long, tapering legs as smooth as marble and marvellous little bathing-costumes of white, pink or blue wool fitting tightly round their thighs, stretched tight where the slight swelling of the stomach began, full of virginity and love.

Nini was all eyes and had lost his tongue, and so it was with the others. They, the beautiful girls from Fiume, did not even

27

notice them but chatted together with their friends and companions in a free and easy way, or played at ball or read under the big umbrellas, all shining with oil. It seemed that they were completely happy, that they needed nothing, that one could not even touch them. Nini and the others lay stretched out on the sand in silence.

A group of girls passed close by, calling like a flock of birds. They ran towards the breakers and threw themselves into the sea. 'Come on,' shouted Nini.

All of one mind, the others got up and followed the girls. They were lingering in the waves, which that day were bigger and higher than usual, letting themselves be rocked in them. Nini approached one of them and called out cheerfully to her in Italian with his thick Friulian accent: 'Wait for me, signorina, or else you'll drown!' The girl gave him an indifferent glance then turned to her companions and burst out laughing. 'What does this donkey want?' she shouted; and together they made for the open sea doing the crawl with a perfect rhythm and swam away towards the mole. Nini dared not go out of his depth. Eligio and Germano could only paddle like dogs, and Basilio could not swim a stroke. They stayed near the shore splashing about in the water then went shamefacedly back up the beach; their cloth pants, which had already made them feel ashamed, were soaked and clinging to them more ridiculously than ever. They rolled in the sand laughing at their bad luck. Then Nini said: 'Shall we go for a walk?' So they ended up at the same place as the day before among the rocks. Behind them the beach was a tumult of shouts and games. Round about the little villas and *pensioni* among the green and the flowers seemed the very picture of serenity and well-being. The sea shimmered endlessly, bathed in sun right up to the marvellous distant blue coasts. And while they walked towards the free beach, the beach for the young and the poor, everything around them was in holiday mood.

They found the boys from the day before and the blond one greeted Nini: 'How's it going, you from Friuli?' he said. 'Well, comrade,' Nini answered with a smile. 'Are the girls from Fiume pretty?' the blond boy asked. 'Not bad,' said Nini as if they no longer had any secrets for him; but he was not in such good spirits as usual. He was thinking of other summers, of bathing in the Tagliamento. Every evening, right after supper they left Ligugnana and went towards Rosa where the branch of the Tagliamento emerged from the stretches of shingle and briar to wash against the right bank, fresh with millet, elders and poplars; and beyond the embankment were the vineyards where the grapes were turning grey and the blocks of cement of the dyke on which to take the sun. All the boys came to Rosa from the villages — Carsara, San Giovanni, Gleris and San Vito — because the Tagliamento was the nicest spot: the water, although deep and green, was so clear that at the bottom you could see the shining pebbles of the shingle. They were all friends back there. Towards evening they would return and stay in the square at Ligugnana until it was time for supper, sitting on the grass or on the steps to chat.

Now as he looked round Nini felt a pang. He went and lay down among the rocks. After a little, the others, leaving the boys from Fiume, came as well and lay down near him in a dejected mood. 'Ah, Madonna, comrades,' sighed Nini. 'The girls may be pretty here,' said Basilio, 'but I like our own better.' 'Just to have Onorina here — or Ines,' said Eligio. 'Or Gemma,' Basilio went on. 'Or that whore, Reina,' added Nini. 'Do you remember that fair when I went into her orchard with her?'

Germano, who had remained silent, suddenly began to hum, his voice gradually becoming louder, one of their favourite songs from Ligugnana: 'Perhaps this will be the last tryst, the last kiss . . . '

The others took up the chorus: Nini and Basilio took the top line, Eligio the second and Germano was bass. On Sunday evenings in the village when they sang in the inns or at the club everyone listened to them.

'Let's sing songs from Friuli and to hell with it!' said Nini. And at the top of his voice he struck up in dialect: 'Oh what a lovely castle at Udine — oh what beautiful young people . . . ' They sang with much feeling although it was a gay *villotta*.

Then they sang a more nostalgic one with all their hearts: 'The cock is crowing — the day is dawning — farewell, my lass — I have to go . . . '

The boys from Fiume had gathered round and stood there listening intently. 'And I sing, sing, sing,' sang Nini, 'but I do

29

not know why – and I sing only – to console myself . . . '

And then the great *villota*, the traditional *villota* of Friuli: 'If you come up here among the crags – where I am buried . . .'

By now they almost had a lump in their throats. They had a strange effect, these songs for Sunday evenings, sung now in the open air in broad daylight beside the sea. But seeing that the boys from Fiume were listening, Nini and the others cast off their melancholy and struck up gay *villottas*. Their voices rang out clearly in the light of the sun which was now settling on the deserted sea to the cry of some gull and the distant noise of voices from the beach. Eligio began: 'I have heard, I have heard – my girl – do psss do psss do psss in the pot . . . ' Now they were all laughing.

For the next two or three days Nini and the others plucked up some courage. Nini hit it off with a girl from Parenzo who worked in a hotel and who introduced her friends to the others. In the end Eligio summed it up: 'Pretty girls, yes, but too much hunger.'

Indeed they had begun their fight against hunger again. After the first two or three days the meals had gone from bad to worse: a couple of spoonfuls of soup and a mouthful of hard, black meat, and even the bread was rationed out. They would get up from the table hungrier than before and went to lie on the sand and brood on their hunger. Then after about three weeks there was something new. In the canteen a supervisor told them they needed cards to eat that very evening.

'What cards?' said Germano.

'Cards,' said the supervisor. 'Without a card you can't eat here.'

Nini was on the point of tears. 'What cards, what fucking cards?' he said.

Germano turned to another worker from Istria who had been at the factory for some time and learned what they had to do. So they at once began a round of the offices: they went through half a dozen in the factory and elsewhere. No one knew anything: everyone was busy. That evening they had no supper.

Next morning they rose early to go to the town hall. There they were ejected from another series of offices. The sultry air of the morning was heavy on their empty stomachs. 'I'm seeing double,' said Nini in a cold sweat.

These were the days when the Cominform was sitting in judgement on Yugoslavia. Great confusion reigned in the city from the factories to the offices, from the shops to the squares. There was the terrified feeling of a city in a state of alarm.

The boys moved slowly away from the town hall in the direction of a little hill at the far end of a square, the burnt green of which shone among the walls of houses and large buildings. They reached the hill and went to stretch themselves out on the benches.

And now? everyone thought silently. Where were they to turn? Just as on the previous evening they had had no supper so today they would have no lunch and then no supper again.

'We're dying of hunger here,' said Eligio. Nini and the others said nothing.

'People die of hunger here because everything is rationed,' Eligio insisted. 'If we don't want to die we have to do something.'

'What then?' said Germano.

'Let's go and steal,' said Nini.

'Yes – with these dogs,' said Germano.

'Disgusting Slavs – there,' said Nini and spat on the ground. At that moment they saw a girl passing the end of a lane.

'Hey, blonde!' shouted Nini.

The blonde girl went straight on, minding her own business, calmly. 'Signorina, signorina!' Nini began to shout.

'Shut up,' muttered Germano. Nini sat up suddenly on the bench where he had been lying. 'No,' he said in an annoyed voice. 'No, I want to ask her something.' He caught up with her. He assumed a serious and courteous air. 'Excuse me, signorina,' he said, 'we're foreigners – we need help.'

The girl looked at him and was reassured by his brown, candid and almost naïve face. 'If I can,' she said. Nini was delighted, turned towards the others and called them. They came and formed a circle round the girl a little timidly. 'Look,' said Nini, 'we've been going round the offices for two days to get ration cards without success. Without ration cards you can't eat so we haven't eaten since midday yesterday. You couldn't give us an idea?' 'Do you work in a factory?' asked the girl. 'Yes, in the torpedo factory.' 'And you are not from these parts — I mean you're not from Istria?' 'We are from Italy,' said Nini. 'Then you have to go to the town hall,' said the girl. 'We've been there,' Nini exclaimed, 'but no one knows anything.' 'That's because you have to go to a special office. Come along,' she added after slight hesitation, 'I'll take you there.' 'Oh thank you, thank you,' shouted Nini with grateful charm. They walked down the hill towards the town hall and on the way they chatted. 'Where are you from?' asked the girl. 'We're from Ligugnana, near Udine,' they replied. Then, each one saying a little, they told the girl their story. They reached the town hall feeling almost light-hearted.

The girl led them across a courtyard and along two or three corridors. 'Here,' she said in front of a broken door, 'it's in there,' and took her leave with a look at Nini. It was the right office but at the little counter window there was an immensely long queue of people. The air was boiling, there was a stink of dirty clothes and sweat. They had come too late — there was no hope of dinner now. The office shut at one. 'We'll come back tomorrow,' said Germano.

And they left to wander about the sun-baked city again looking for something to eat. They went into various shops but there was nothing without a ration card even if you were dying. Now they were finished by the heat and the hunger, so they decided to buy at an immense price a jar of jam, the only foodstuff unrationed. In a minute the jar had been cleaned out.

With the sweetness of the jam in their empty stomachs they stretched out on their beds. No one said anything. Through the shutters the high sun burst humming into the room along with stagnant noises and the breathing of the sea, which was loud but damped by the distance, making the silence still denser.

No one was sleeping, yet no one wished to speak or had the courage to speak. They were silent, sweating, each one with his own hunger.

Suddenly it was Basilio who broke the silence.

'Boys, I'm going home,' he said. The others made no reply.

'We suffer too much hunger here,' Basilio went on.

'Yes, let's get away from here,' said Eligio, who had not been well those last few days, with a sob almost rising in his throat.

'Hey, comrades,' said Nini, 'what's the matter with you?'

'We've had a bellyful,' said Basilio.

'And what are you going to do?' muttered Germano.

'Go away from here,' said Basilio. 'I'm going.' Eligio leapt to his feet. 'I won't stay another day,' he cried. He had managed to overcome the emotion which had had him by the throat; now he talked more freely but seemed to have made his mind up. Nini and Germano on the other hand continued to say nothing, stretched out on their beds, and for some minutes silence and the oppressive heat fell on the room once more.

'I'm going – do you understand?' Eligio began again, 'I don't want to die of hunger. Do you really think we will get ration cards tomorrow? If we want to kid ourselves they'll perhaps give us them in three or four days. And meantime will we live on jam? And the money? And then when we have the cards we'll just die bit by bit with the food they give us at the torpedo factory. At home you're sure of a plate of beans and polenta even if you don't work. No, at home you're never without a few beans, a bit of polenta and a slice of salami – never.'

'In Italy you may not work,' Basilio went on, 'but at least they say that in Italy you don't die of hunger. We've seen some bad times at home, but we never dreamt of hunger like this. Comrades, for my part I'm going. We'll both go, Eligio.'

Germano said: 'Let's try to hold out a few more days. Maybe when we have the cards they'll give us better food to eat.'

Eligio replied to him violently, almost weeping once more: 'You stay then, you stay. We've held out for a month and a half and it's got worse and worse, damn it. That's enough. I'm going home.'

'Great,' said Nini, 'and how will you cross the frontier? We managed it coming but how? By accident. If it had been up to that man we'd still be back there eating roots. Do you think it will all go right another time? And then if the Italians caught us – well, we would still be at home but if these bastards catch you goodness knows what they might do to you.'

'They'll kill you,' said Germano.

'Communism may be great,' said Nini. 'That's an idea I've got firmly in my head and will have till I die – but these bastards!'

'You can say what you like,' Eligio interrupted him. 'I'll even risk rabies, but death by hunger is the worst death there is. And then in any case they shoot you in the back as you cross the frontier and amen.'

'It was easy to come here,' Germano repeated, 'but going back — '

'It feels like a hundred years since I saw Italy,' said Nini hoarsely.

'It's a long, long way,' said Germano.

'What a lot of nonsense,' exclaimed Basilio. 'You take the train and in a night you're at Gorizia.'

'All right,' Nini cried suddenly. 'I'm with you. I'm leaving too.' And he rose to his feet as if the train were standing ready at the door.

'What about you, Germano?' asked Eligio.

'Do you want me to stay here alone?' said Germano. 'If you three go back to Italy so do I.'

That same night they took the train at half-past one for Gorizia. In the afternoon they had got their suitcases ready and had bought jam and a little bread.

It was an old Italian train with signs of bombing, all peeling and windowless. They found a third-class compartment to themselves and settled down in it. Eligio and Nini stretched out on the seats, Germano and Basilio on the floor. But they could not sleep. The train ran along snorting, rattling, shaking, in continuous curves through the mountains of Istria which were stuck against the moonless night like ghosts. Rivers and sea disappeared behind them as if swallowed up in an unreal light. And it seemed as if the train ran aimlessly through this territory, which was neither Italian nor Slav — its only goal the darkness of the night.

'Goodbye, Fiume,' said Nini with his hands folded under his head. 'Goodbye, Tito.'

In spite of the uncertainty of the future, towards dawn there was Italy, and Yugoslavia disappeared slowly behind them with its hunger and poverty.

'When we have our revolution,' said Germano, 'things won't be like they are here.'

'Ah,' exclaimed Nini, 'meantime we're going to eat Christian

Democrat beans. Milio was right,' he said to himself with his eyes turned towards the black ceiling of the carriage, 'Milio was right to get his papers to go to Switzerland.'

The train stopped suddenly after giving two or three piercing whistles which echoed in the emptiness of a little valley. Nini went to the window and saw a station. On the side of a hill one could glimpse a milky row of houses. 'A village,' he said.

The carriage doors banged. There was a great tramping of feet, shouts, calls, collisions. The train appeared to be emptying.

'What's happening?' said Eligio. Nini opened the door and got down on to the track. 'Everyone's getting out,' he shouted.

They got their luggage in haste and got down too. The whole crowd had gathered on the platform, making a great noise, moving about. It was still pitch dark – it couldn't even be three yet. Nini and the others got into the middle of the crowd, which was made up almost entirely of refugees. The train for Gorizia was supposed to arrive in half an hour. The boys waited seated on their luggage.

The new train was packed. The crowd attacked it furiously, fighting in the dark. Some got on to the footboards, clinging to the handles, others sat on the buffers, and a few climbed up on to the roof. The children and women who had been left on the ground shouted. More than half the people had not been able to get on and were running up and down the tracks in indescribable confusion. Suddenly Nini noticed that he had been left alone. He began to look around among the people but could not see his comrades. Then he began to go up and down the train shouting: 'Eligio, Germano!' His voice could not even be heard among the chaos on the tracks. Five minutes passed, ten, quarter of an hour. By now those that were in were in and people no longer even tried to cling to the doors but shouted and protested. Nini in desperation continued to go up and down, looking and shouting almost without noticing any more: 'Eligio, Germano!'

'They're putting on another coach,' Germano's voice said suddenly behind him. 'Ah, there you are,' Nini cried happily. 'And the others?' 'I don't know,' shouted Germano. They ran towards the back of the train. A new coach was indeed being attached and they were among the first to rush in. There they found Eligio as well. But Basilio was lost for a short while.

35

They travelled all the rest of the night until the dawn shone white on Istria. The light gained the naked peaks of the mountains; the sun was born, hot and round, and from the horizon poured into the train a chalk-white light. Nini reopened his eyes amid the chaos that crammed the compartments and corridors. 'Boys!' he cried. The others woke up, yawning, and after a little the train stopped.

It was a lonely little station. Almost everyone got out there. The boys looked about them not knowing what to do. Among those getting out there was a young boy of thirteen and Nini turned to him. 'Are we near the frontier here?' he whispered to him. 'Yes,' said the boy. 'Let's get off,' shouted Nini. The others were uncertain. 'Come on, let's get off,' Nini repeated and seizing his luggage went after the boy. The others followed him. On the platform Nini started talking again to the boy, who was alone. 'Tell me,' he said, 'how do you get close to the frontier?'

'Today it's difficult,' the boy answered. 'It's a holiday. You can't get there.'

'So we should get back on to the train?'

'Not this one – it doesn't go to Gorizia,' said the boy.

'So how can we get to Gorizia?' 'It's a holiday today – nothing's going there.' 'So what can we do?' 'You can walk to the other station and wait there for the train to Gorizia. I'll go with you if you like.' 'Oh thanks,' said Nini. 'Good boy.'

Nini took his arm and they left the station together, turning a corner before entering the village by a dusty road that was lost to sight along the side of the hill, which was all stone and without shade in the fiery sun. In little more than an hour they reached the other station but the train would not come through before midday. They threw themselves down on the ground to sleep in a grassy piece of open ground near the station. Later they took the train and towards evening arrived in Gorizia.

They got out under the platform roof in the midst of a crowd of police. But the confusion of the refugees, with women shouting and babies crying, was so great that they got lost among it.

'Courage, boys,' said Germano quietly.

'Lord, grant us this favour,' said Nini. They came out along with the line of refugees without anyone saying anything. They were free – in Italy. In the station square swallows were flying, people were chatting, you could smell the scent of damp earth, of hearths. Nini felt as if he were in Ligugnana at the time of day when the peasants come back from the fields on the haywain and the kitchens are full of people talking, quarrelling, singing, while the little ones bring the animals to drink at the trough by the pump and the girls comb their hair before taking the milk to the dairy. The village square becomes lively, assumes an almost holiday air with the good smell of polenta in the warm evening air and the first lights coming on here and there. There in the village by the station the little stone houses with courtyards and byres, mulberry-trees, vines, the sides of the country road were exactly like those of Ligugnana or San Giovanni, even if the mountains were closer. Even people's dialect was almost the same. And far off, beyond the last houses, beyond the expanse of the city, you could make out the course of the Isonzo between the mountains and the plain – the Isonzo with its shingle bed and its channels of blue and transparent water so like those of the Tagliamento.

'We're home, boys,' said Nini cheerfully breathing deeply the air of the villages of Friuli.

'Let's go and drink a glass,' said Basilio.

'Maybe two,' shouted Nini.

'Go easy, boys,' said Germano. 'It's not said that we're through yet.'

They went into an inn, but no sooner had they entered than they saw that it was a police post. They just managed to leave before someone arrested them. They cut down by a little side road, jumped a ditch and got into a field of maize. They wanted to eat the little bread and jam they had left before going on. They stayed half an hour in their hiding-place among the corn-cobs on the cool upturned earth. Then they came out and began to walk along the road towards the town. But, unexpectedly, round a corner they saw a big patrol of police coming towards them. They could neither turn back nor throw themselves into the fields beyond the ditch.

They were arrested and taken at once to the police post from which they were moved on to prison in Gorizia. They stayed in prison a fair time. It would not be until September that they reached home.

V

'We arrived in Switzerland at night,' Milio began to tell his friends, 'and the station at Brigue was all lit up. Behind it you could see the little town with the mountains that surrounded it – beautiful, high and full of little lights.

'I stayed in Brigue until the morning and then immediately phoned Fribourg and my friend, Lina, to tell her to wait for me because I was leaving Brigue in less than half an hour. So at midday I arrived at Fribourg. I got out of the train and left the station looking for the young lady because we had agreed that she would take me to Salvenach, which was where I had to go. After I had been waiting for a while I suddenly saw her coming towards me – her and her sister Catina. We embraced affectionately like good friends and went straight to their house.

'There they offered me sweets and beer. They asked after my family and all their relations in Rosa. But it was already late, five in the evening and, as agreed, Lina had come to take me to the village where I was to go to work, which was not far from Fribourg.

'We got out at a station called Cressier, from which we had to walk for a kilometre. But you could already see Salvenach up there. We set out along a fine little tarred road surrounded by fruit-trees. In the distance we could see a fine house and I said to the young lady: "I wish that was the one I had to go to!"

'We arrived in the square of the little village. There we found an old man and we asked him: "Where is Walter Berninger's house?" And he said politely: "The first house on the right."

Then we turned back the way he had pointed, and it was the very same little villa as we had seen before! I was very pleased; it was so pretty up there – a real house for ladies and gentlemen. But there was no one there – only a big dog. I stood where I was because it frightened me a bit; but my friend waited for Signor Berninger, walking up and down in the garden without paying any attention to it.

'Suddenly we saw a man of about fifty and the young lady asked him in French if he was Walter Berninger; and it was he. He asked us both in and offered us food, drink and cigarettes. You can't imagine what a welcome it was. After a bit I went to see the girl off and thanked her very much for her trouble. And then it was supper-time. The boss called me into the kitchen and I saw the table ready laid. But I was cast down right away when I saw that there was no tablecloth on the table and a soup that seemed to be made of vegetable marrow, and coffee and milk without salt or sugar. That was what there was to eat. The boss saw I was a bit glum and to cheer me up a little sent for a couple of other Italians who had been living in Salvenach for a year now. We talked about all sorts of things; they told me to cheer up and said: "You'll get used to it gradually, come on."

'I didn't get on very well with my boss because he didn't want to pay me the agreed wage; but everybody in the village respected me because I was a good worker. But there were lots of things I didn't understand: why were they so rude and hard to me when I had done my duty? People aren't like that in our parts. But one evening I had the chance to talk to a certain Signorina Leich who lived in the village where I worked. She was German by birth but had studied and had been in Italy several times and liked Italians. She spoke Italian and many other languages. She very kindly explained all sorts of things to me about my boss because she knew him. He owned a lot of land but it was all mortgaged to the government and so, since he couldn't pay me every month, he looked serious and gloomy.

'Things got worse from day to day with continual unpleasant-nesses; even the village was sorry I had landed up in a family with its affairs in such a bad state. By now it had been fixed that I would go home at Christmas; but for me the time did not pass. On the 3rd of November at Morat there was a huge fair. My bosses had gone there and so I was left alone at home.

'In the afternoon I went to graze the cows in the meadow where the railway passed. I was quietly looking after the beasts when soon I saw a pretty blonde girl arrive from the other side of the railway embankment; she had cows too. I knew her already; she was from Cressier, the village next to mine. I went towards her and we had a nice talk sitting by the railway line.

'She knew me by sight too. But she kept on reading a book and being serious while I was expecting . . . Suddenly I asked this beautiful Germaine: "What are you reading?"

'And she answered very nicely: "The Two Little Orphans". We already seemed to be in love with each other. So I made my declaration as best I could in French: "Germaine, je vous aime." And she took what I said affectionately. We parted with an understanding. After that on the evenings when I was free I saw a lot of her and we went dancing or to the cinema like a proper engaged couple.

'One day my boss said to me: "The next fair at Libistorf is a big one. Go there because it is interesting especially for you Italians."

'So six or seven of us Italians got together and on the day of the fair we set out for Libistorf. It was about five kilometres from Salvenach and happened to be one of the villages I hadn't been to. On the way we kept along the side of a wood and on the other you could see the lush green valley. Suddenly we reached Libistorf which was very small but all made up of beautiful little villas although the inhabitants were peasants. I liked the village a lot because it was rich and different from the others, with little lakes on one side and on the other beautiful pines and firs.

'When we got to the centre of the village everyone was anxious for the fair to begin but it wasn't ready yet. Meantime we Italians sat on the side of the ditch to eat fruit and said to each other: "This is a good place to be because the procession must pass right in front of us."

'About an hour later the procession began to make the first round of the village. At the head there was a man beating a drum who walked backwards facing the company. The drum was being beaten to make two of the finest horses in the village, ridden by two jockeys dressed in old-fashioned military uniforms, dance in time. After them came a big pine-tree twenty-five metres long with very thick branches drawn by eight finely decked-out horses. In the middle of this pine a boy was standing covered with little pine twigs, holding forth all the time, but we could not understand him because he was speaking German, though it seemed that he was saying funny things to make the people laugh. Behind that came a wedding between a pretty girl dressed in white and a young man all in black. Then a great company singing and behind them again a cart with four badly dressed boys planting pines and another with young women, also badly dressed, harvesting maize, one in each corner of the cart. Then came young men with racing-bicycles done up in paper of different colours. Behind them you could see a lorry laden with pails and a herd of the finest cows in the place, all picked, with a bell on each one's neck hanging down to the ground and, last of all, two hunters dressed in an old-fashioned way with a gun on their shoulders and a dog each, little white ones.

'In the village there was a great crowd with the girls dressed in peasant costume and little flags in their hands. You kept hearing the shots from the shooting galleries and in the middle of the square among all the noise, there was a man on a bench with a round tray in his hand; in the middle of the tray stood a litre of white wine and two glasses, one on each side, and he made them spin round very fast without letting them fall and all the time he held forth in German to amuse people. Finally, towards evening, there was a great dance in a lovely hall, you should have seen!'

'The peasants in Switzerland are very different from here,' Milio went on. 'They have better chances because there are hardly any big families like ours and so they can sell almost all their crops. Their houses are much nicer than ours – and what byres – they look like toys! And then everyone has a radio and a phone in their house. But the big difference from us is the food. Although we're poor, we eat like the richest of them. It seems to me that they are harder and have much less humanity than us. Even if they go to school till sixteen yet they are less intelligent and then they have meanness in their blood. It's bad luck for the people who have to work for them. Because they are people who don't bother much about themselves or others. They keep on working without ever getting tired, even in the rain, and in summer under the high sun

41

in the middle of the afternoon. There's no one over fifty who doesn't have arthritic pains and they think it isn't work that does it! In the evening, after working without a break, they don't go to have a gossip in the street as we do; they keep to themselves in their own houses. But that was fine for us because there was less chance of being seen when we went walking with the pretty blondes.

'My boss was someone with no common sense and he let his interests go to wrack and ruin. He was very spoilt. He liked to eat well and to drink and smoke without doing anything. The only thing he was interested in was his wife. He was criticized a lot in the village because he didn't work and had big debts as well, so that what he owned only looked as if it was his while in fact it was already owned by others. He had a farm of forty hectares and fifteen beasts in his byre and it only kept going because of the work of two farmhands: myself and my friend, Ernst Gubler, who was Swiss, but lived in the north in the city of Alten. My boss was German and in Salvenach they all talked his language, German. He had got married twenty years before and had four children called Peter, Cartli, Hans and Anna Marì. They were all Protestants in the family but although they were Protestants they were very religious. Every Sunday they had to walk four kilometres to go to Mass because at Salvenach there wasn't one of their churches.

'Luckily my mate liked me, for very often the boss was fed up because things were going badly and then he took it out on us farmhands; but it was no use because Ernst, who spoke his language, pointed out to thim that it was his own fault and so I got off too. Signor Berninger was always a very reserved man and didn't confide much in anybody. In Salvenach there were four families of Berningers all related to one another; they were the oldest families in the village and were very well off. My boss's misfortune was that he had lost his father, who was a member of parliament, when he was very young and because of his inexperience hadn't been able to run his property well and now it was in ruins.

'Salvenach must have had about five hundred inhabitants. The moment you left the station at Cressier you saw it all along the side of the hill.

'In Switzerland almost all the villages are built on the tops of hills. But for me Salvenach was the prettiest of all.

'From Cressier you could see its little white houses and behind them the slope of the mountain full of pines and villas. It was on the main road eight kilometres from Fribourg and three from the lake of Morat. The other villages I had got to know were far from the road in open country. Seeing Salvenach appear in the distance on the road with its line of fine houses you would have said it had a lot more than five hundred inhabitants.

'Going towards Fribourg from Salvenach the road looked very different than it did going towards Morat. On the Fribourg side all you saw was the green of the countryside and to right and left, along the road, there were quite a few villages: Cormond, Iois and many others. Whereas towards Morat all you had to do was get on your bicycle and you didn't need to pedal until the village square.

'On that side the view was very beautiful. You saw little clumps of wood with winding paths leading into them, covered with white, shiny gravel, and here and there rustic benches on which the Swiss rested when they were out walking in summer with their rucksacks on their backs — especially lovers.

'The fields where I worked stretched round the village for a square kilometre on either side of the main road and reached almost to the other villages, always surrounded where it was flat by a huge wood.

'What a beautiful little city Fribourg is! I could never have imagined such beauty. The moment I entered the city for the first time I was filled with joy to see those wide squares, such clean streets, and hotels, pastry-shops, shop windows — any number of them. The buildings weren't as high as those in our cities but they had wonderful cornices painted with flowers and patterns in the traditional Swiss way. In Fribourg I found the young people handsome and athletic. The young women were rather tall, slim, with long wavy blonde hair. One day I was invited to play the accordion in Fribourg at the house of some friends of my boss's daughter and then I saw just how traditional Switzerland is. The girls had *jambon* — that's pork — for their snack and wore dresses in the Fribourg style. Their shoes were black and their socks white. Then they had little maroon aprons all embroidered from the

43

shoulder to the waist. Little gilt chains hung down everywhere and on their heads they had lovely gauze bonnets tied into a peak.'

'The girls in Switzerland are much more advanced than here. And my boss's daughter . . . Ah, I'll always remember her!

'One evening after supper I had to go to Cressier to fetch two big suitcases from the station because Peter, who was a student in Lausanne, had arrived. With these two heavy suitcases I had to walk all the way from the station to the village. And there was a good hill to climb because Salvenach is one of the highest villages. When I was halfway there I stopped to rest and smoke half a cigarette. Suddenly I saw down below near the station three or four girls coming towards the village. I stopped and waited for them thinking: "Perhaps I know them and so they'll help me to carry the weight of these cases."

'They came up and it was just as I thought . . . I knew all three of them from the day I was in Fribourg. Without me asking they took the cases and asked me: "Hello – where do you work?"

' "In Salvenach," I replied, "at the Berningers'."

' "You're in luck," said the girls laughing, "because there's a pretty girl there."

' "Don't laugh," I said, "she's my boss's daughter."

'But from then on I began to think about Anna Marì, my boss's daughter, whereas before the three girls talked to me about her she hadn't even entered my head. The Berninger family where I worked was made up of the father, the mother and the four children, three sons and a daughter, Anna Marì. The land belonged to the father but he had given it to his son Cartli to farm. Hans worked a long way from the village in a wood, whereas Peter was a scholar, spoke Italian and came home from school every fortnight. Hans came home every two or three months. Anna Marì did the housework and when there was a lot of work in the fields she came to help us too.

'One fine evening at the beginning of the month Peter was home on holiday. I had started playing the accordion in my room. Suddenly in came Anna Marì, Peter and the son of the local teacher. On the spur of the moment they organized a little party. Each of them began to dance a bit with Anna Marì. Then they went and got sparkling wine, chocolate and other sweets. So in a couple of hours we were all a bit merry. But the moment came when we had to break up — in fact Peter had to go into the village. But I and this other friend of mine, Armando, stayed on in the room for about an hour chatting. My friend knew Anna Marì pretty well and said as much to me with a wink. He helped me to do both myself and her a good turn, and while he looked out of the window at the fine starry evening I said softly to her, "Trè joli, trè joli" and kissed and cuddled her.

'Anna Marì was a blonde girl, a bit fat, not very tall but pale-faced with a beautiful smooth white complexion. She did her hair so that it was taken back and fell in waves on her neck. That evening she was wearing a white wool pullover. She had been telling me for a while: "You are very nice." And, inside, I liked her a lot but didn't let on to the rest of the family because I knew they would have been jealous. The young woman thought I was nice because she heard me talk to everyone in the same way. I took care to be nice to people so that everyone up there would like me.

'I hadn't understood Anna Marì at first. She was the one of all the girls who was nicest to me but I didn't want to think about it and did not even know what she thought of me.

'But one time there had been difficulties between us so that we had almost quarrelled and didn't get on well after that. In fact from then on we hardly spoke to each other any more. The first difficulty arose at a dance. At a party in Salvenach an Italian called Olivieri had asked her to dance with him and she had replied that she didn't dance with Italians because her father didn't like them.

'Me, when I heard what she said, seeing I was an Italian and worked for her father, I got depressed. And the next day I told her brother, Cartli, all about it. And to tell the truth I told him almost in tears because I felt very offended and depressed. "Why did Anna Marì behave like that?" I asked him. "Maybe I'm better mannered than you Swiss think," I told Cartli, "and the women think we are all good-for-nothings but it's not true and maybe we're more honest than you Swiss."

' "Ah, my friend," Cartli replied, "don't go running after Anna Marì because she's a child, believe me, she's a child — a child."

'Cartli was the brother Anna Marì didn't get on with; for her Peter was the only one. The second difficulty she and I had was another time when Anna Marì got angry over her sister-in-law who liked me too much. Cartli's wife was called Cecilia; she was still young and she had grown very fond of me. Every time she went down to the shop she bought me sweets. I didn't understand her very well either, but she behaved very oddly with me and was silly to bring me a little present every time. Anna Marì was jealous because she was in love with me and she went about the village saying – to Armando and the other youngsters – that I had a good time in Cartli's house because I got on well with Cecilia.

'So hearing about this gossip I went and complained to Anna Marì and told her she had behaved badly. So from then on she stopped saying I was nice. And I tried to do my best at work without bothering about her and tried to get the others to like me.

'The evening that we had that party we talked to each other for the first time for weeks. Then the time came when Armando said he had to go home; so very quietly, both of the same mind, we left the kitchen so that her brother wouldn't hear us. The moment we were outside Armando said good-night but Anna Marì didn't want to go to bed yet and said she felt this was the nicest evening of her life because she was with a young Italian who was kissing her. She led me out through the stable and we went for a walk in the fields. This pretty blonde was very attractive but at the same time I was unsure because I kept thinking about so many things. I said to her: "Suppose your brothers found us? What would happen to me?"

'But she wasn't worried and I didn't know what to do because, feeling that girl in my arms, I had a tremendous desire to make love to her. Then she encouraged me a little, telling me her brother Cartli who was sleeping didn't worry about her and that if Peter saw us he wouldn't say anything because he understood about young people.

'Walking along very quietly we found a nice spot where we sat down to rest with our two loving hearts next to each other.

'The house where I worked was one of the very last in Salvenach which, like all Swiss villages, was on the very top of a

46

little hill with the countryside stretching below it. From the door of the Berningers' house you could see at your feet the other houses in the village, the hill and all the woods round the fields.

'Anna Marì and me, having left the courtyard, had gone down through the village, had crossed the railway and had arrived under the first pines. And there in the shadow we found our nook.

'I ran my hands all over her but not too far down because I was afraid to make a mistake and offend her. But I was wrong; all my friends told me afterwards that she wanted it and that I could have done anything I liked with her. We only kissed and said all those things true lovers say to each other.

' "I'm not going to stay at home any more," said Anna Marì, "I'm leaving to work in Fribourg."

' "If you find me a job with you," I said to her, "then we'll get married . . . Si toi cherger du travail plus joli, moi travailler avec toi – moi avec toi – aprè nous marrier, et aprè nous seron trè content toujour – promener, moi avec toi – dancer – et aprè nous aurion de garçons . . . "

' "Oui, oui, moi faire le possible," said Anna Marì.

' "But don't let your parents see you being so nice to me," I impressed on her with all my heart. And in fact I had noticed that her father and mother when we were together kept watching us and had their ears pricked to hear what we said. But the day I spoke to Cartli about the dance I had also pointed out to him the way Papa Walter behaved. "There's no need for Signor Berninger to keep watching like that. If I and Anna Marì talk to each other a lot it is because I want to hear French words and maybe she wants to hear Italian ones. We Italians are not like you think."

'And Cartli had told it all to his father, Walter, and his mother, Adelaide. Then one day the boss sent me to buy a couple of bottles of beer. When I came back with the bottles I went to his room. "Come on," he said, "let's drink the beer together." I understood that he wanted to say something to me, clearly in connection with what I had told Cartli about Anna Marì. We went into his room which was well furnished, full of expensive, polished furniture. There we drank the beer and ate biscuits as well. Then he took me to see the other room too, where there were all his mementoes. On the wall two or three diplomas were

47

hanging and in a little glass box a gold medal he had earned because he had been member of a choir for forty years.

' "Ah," I said, "I'd only need a quarter of all there is here to be able to get married."

' "Drink up, my friend," said the boss.

' "And Signora Adelaide?" I asked.

'The old man went down to call her and so all three of us chatted together. They were very polite and I understood that they wanted to tell me something. When we drank the beer we looked at each other right in the eye because that is the custom there — it was a good job I knew this otherwise I would have seemed rude. I knew because I was very friendly with Armando and one evening we had gone drinking with a group of friends. We were drinking beer and while we drank I was looking round. Then a boy came up to me and asked if I was angry with him. "No," I said and another Italian who was with us warned me that the Swiss look into each other's eyes when they drink. So that evening with old Walter I knew about this custom and while I drank I looked at him and he looked at me and smiled, and so did Mamma Adelaide. We did not say anything about Anna Marì and the gossip at the dance; but I understood that it was about this that the old couple wanted to talk to me. So without saying a word we forgave each other and made things up.

'This was why I was now very frightened that Anna Marì might give her parents a hint that she had been in the wood with me.

'From the nook where we had been hidden to our house was about a kilometre but that kilometre was as long as ten for anyone who had to walk it alone because it was all uphill. We walked along arm in arm — we hadn't much to be happy about — but all we thought about was how marvellous love is. But in the end our walk under the stars and the moon that shone down on us tired us and so the last bit of the climb was hard going as if that hill had been a mountain. It was getting on for the early hours of Monday; the moment had stolen up on us; the parting was very long and Anna Marì, before saying good-night, gave me twenty or thirty little kisses on the lips. From then on we still talked nicely to each other about lots of things but not very often and not about love any more.'

'In the evening I was almost always overcome by great sadness. I remembered Rosa which at that time of day was so beautiful and full of life. Everyone was tired from the work in the fields but at the same time there was so much jollity all round. My little brothers would be loading the milk-cans on the handlebars of their bicycles and pedalling off happily whistling towards the village square. On the main road, summer or winter, there was always a coming and going of floats or carts or bicycles on their way to Rosa or Gruaro, and the women, lighting the fire or gathering in the clothes set out to dry in the courtyards, would talk to one another, shouting and laughing. That was a good time of day; we young men washed ourselves at the pump while the old men or the little boys took the animals to drink and then we went to change, for in our villages there is always a bit of fun towards evening.

'But in Switzerland at that time of day it suddenly got cold and dark and everyone withdrew into their fine houses.

'I remember that one of these evenings the boss said to me: "Gabli can't come to work for us any more and so you will go with the dogs to the dairy with the milk." I had to say "Yes" but I was very depressed by this task. I wasn't used to it and I was ashamed to do that job. I didn't know what to give them to eat to make them friendly. They snarled, barked and never stood still. But I stroked them and harnessed them patiently, then I yoked them to the little cart. The dairy was a good distance away and that evening it was drizzling. Before I went down to the village the boss called from the door: "If you know how, you can get on to the cart too."

'I set off without worrying and after about a hundred metres jumped on to the cart to make these wretched animals pull me. Out of habit they were going towards the dairy without being driven, but suddenly at the bottom of the road they saw some other dogs and began to run after them, barking like demons.

'I wasn't able to hold them back and after a long chase past the first houses in the village with people shouting and laughing, I, the dogs, and the milk-cans ended up by overturning in the ditch. At that moment Anna Marì was cycling along the street in her white pullover and, seeing me go head over heels, began to laugh, still pedalling, and without turning round.

'The next day there was a party and I and some companions went to dance in Cormond. The party was in the midst of the wood and I danced with Anna Marì and Lilian. Then I went off on my own and they stayed on at the dance till late.

'The Berningers' house was empty when I got back and shining like a mirror. I harnessed the dogs and went to the dairy. Salvenach, too, was almost empty. The young people were having fun at the dance in the woods. In Salvenach there were only the old people getting drunk on beer. I was alone in my bosses' house as evening fell and the little lights lit up on all the hills around and the stars were beginning to shine in the sky which was clear and fresh because of the rain the day before. I was in my little room on the ground floor near the kitchen, and I was so sad that I almost felt like crying. When it was getting late and all the rest of the family had gone to bed I heard noises in the kitchen and became aware that it was Anna Marì and Lilian with their two suitors chatting among themselves. Then I heard them preparing a bite to eat and drinking coffee. Without giving them any further thought, I began to drop off to sleep but their constant talk kept waking me up. From my room, because of a stove-chimney, I could see if it was light or dark in the kitchen, so as I knew the trick I was all ears to see what would happen. Time passed quickly for them and from my room I could see that in the kitchen the light was still on and heard all four of them talking away in low voices and Anna Marì saying: "Talk quietly because the farmhand can hear us and maybe he has just gone to bed." Then suddenly I noticed that the light had been put out and that everything was quiet in the kitchen. But I heard the benches creaking. I could not sleep and could have wept for rage. In the morning, when I saw Anna Marì I looked at her and laughed but she had no idea why. It so happened that I had to work in the house that day and towards midday Lilian also came past and kept on chatting to Anna Marì about the lovely evening they had had. Suddenly I said: "Did you have a nice night?" and they stood there with their mouths open and wanted to know if I had listened to what they had been saying. I said: "It so happens I didn't sleep last night and I heard you fine. But it's your business."

'To make me angry Anna Marì, instead of denying it, told a

story that laid it on thick. But Lilian laughed because she and I got on well just as on all the other evenings. Anna Marì got very heated but gradually she calmed down and in the end said to me: "You'd better not gossip about it."

'She had been very much in love but the fault was mine if we did not go on because on the evening of our walk in the wood I had not had the courage to do with her what she wanted; but by now I was fed up with Anna Marì and I wasn't worried that things had finished the way they had.

'On many evenings, at sunset, she would come up the path because during the day she went to help her cousin, and I sat there writing letters on the window-sill looking out to the fields.

'Then she would sit in the courtyard on a heap of logs and we talked like friends. To tell the truth I was slightly angry when I saw that she had a date with someone else. One Sunday when they were all out and I had stayed alone in the house to save money I noticed that she was coming up the hill with another boy. She had got engaged to him and took him up into her bedroom. Next morning I said to her: "Ah, Anna Marì, ça va bien en ault a fair l'amour!"

' "Oui, oui," she replied as if to annoy me.

' "Eh, bien, chère Anna Marì," I said to her, "pour moi en fait rien! Pour moi en Italie c'est une amie plus jolie que toi, plus jolie, plus jolie." '

VI

One evening at the beginning of October, although it was
pouring with rain and was already late, many lights were still on
in San Giovanni. In the inns the doors were open and threw
gleaming patches of light on to the flooded streets and into the
shadows. Across them passed the customers, bowed under
umbrellas or covered with sacks, their feet sinking deep in the
muddy ruts.

Hardly anyone had gone to the evening Mass; the big church
and the square remained empty. Borgo Romans, in front of
them, was lost in the torrents of rain which seemed almost like
winter and the same even went for Borgo Monte, except for some
movement near the bar. The unusual activity concerned only
Borgo Braida, the central street of San Giovanni, round the
workers' club.

The doors and windows of the inn, which incidentally did not
have shutters, were wide open and threw on to the street and the
roofs of the little shabby houses near by beams of yellow light to
which were added the voices and the din from inside. Inside, in
fact, in the two rooms of the ground floor and upstairs in the
other two which were the Party offices, an exceptional crowd of
men had gathered, as well as women too, which was unusual.
The rooms, whether upstairs or down, were filled with smoke,
for the people had been gathered there for a long time. In fact,
the meeting was just about to finish. Pieri Susanna, the secretary
of the branch, was talking seriously near the bar with a young
man from the union who had come specially from Pordenone to

take part in the meeting and now, before leaving, was making final arrangements. Round the pair were the older men, either from the Party branch or from the agricultural union, who with a certain seriousness were listening – their faces burnt by the air and wine – to the talk of the two officials. The others were talking too, seated at the little tables or standing bunched together so as to fill the two little rooms from the very pavement, gleaming with puddles.

Upstairs the meeting of the Young Pioneers was still going on; up there too, unusually, there was a great deal of seriousness and almost of reflection.

The young people were sitting on benches or standing along the walls smoking in their heavy jackets or in overalls that smelt strongly of water and litter.

There was Eligio, still pale and thin, after the hardships of life in Yugoslavia, with his skin stretched over his jaws like a man with tuberculosis, and his blue eyes which seemed to melt from time to time, but as cheerful as ever, always ready to laugh and sing. There was his cousin, Jacu; there were his younger brothers, Onorino and Livo, who had grown since we last saw them even if they were still in short trousers, and their mates, Chini, Ivano, Rino and all the others from the various quarters of San Giovanni.

That evening the young people from Casarsa, from Sila, had also met there. And even four or five girls from Borgo Romans had come.

The secretary had just finished speaking but they still stayed on together, partly waiting for the rain to stop, partly to talk about things and to make final arrangements. But the boys were shy. Eligio, who was near the rickety table under the crucifix and the portrait of Stalin, asked with a blush: 'Haven't you anything to say? Come on, speak up!' The rest looked at one another and said nothing.

'What do you want stupid people like us to say?' shouted his brother Onorino with a laugh. 'It's OK like this.'

Livio, the third brother, the youngest one, who was standing in the corner near the door, took two steps to the wall opposite, where behind the cupboard the flag was leaning, and with a laugh took it out from among the loose plaster and unrolled it: 'Tomorrow you will fly at the head of the Young Pioneers of San

Giovanni,' he said. 'Good luck!' The rest laughed in amusement at his words.

'Tomorrow,' a teenager from Braida continued, taking hold of it, 'we'll stick you under the nose of the Pitottis and Spilimbergos.'

'Let them get a good smell of you,' shouted Onorino and he shook a fold hard. The flag unfurled completely and almost covered the heads of those close by. 'Long live our beautiful banner,' shouted Eligio and began to shake it gaily.

Outside it continued to pour and you would have thought that the whole district along the Tagliamento, from the foothills to the sea, must be almost lifeless under that storm: the lonely villages, the unpassable roads, the abandoned fields. Instead, as in all the villages of the district, there was the same stir, the same unusual shining lights. Like Eligio and Jacu in San Giovanni, Milio too had gone to the meeting at his Party branch in Rosa and Nini in Lingugnana, where it seemed as if everyone was up and about as if it were the busy eve of some festival.

The delegates from all the branches of the Gruara area had been summoned and it was down there that the leading members from Pordenone and even from Udine had gathered. The Party branch had its offices in the same big building where the dance-hall was. The place for leaving bicycles was packed full like a Sunday evening under the dusty electric lights.

The secretary, Pieri Susanna, should have been at Ligugnana too had the rain not prevented him; in his place his son, Mariano, had gone down and in fact it was for him – with the latest instructions – that everybody was waiting. The others were taking the opportunity to drink an extra glass in the expectation of success next day and ended up by starting to sing. Young and old were gathered round the bar; Eligio had brought down the flag.

Only towards eleven did it begin to stop raining, and those who lived a long way away gathered at the door of the workers' club to breathe the harsh damp air and to inspect the sky which was still swollen with clouds which sailed through it in confusion. Every so often a gust of sirocco caused another downpour of rain on San Giovanni, shaking the red signboard with the badge of the Party which hung at the door of the workers' club.

Defying the last outbursts of the storm those from Casarsa and Bosco set off on their bicycles along the muddy road, singing. Shortly afterwards Pieri Susanna's son arrived from Ligugnana without any counter-orders for the following day and so the rest also set out for home, continuing to talk excitedly through the sleep and winter silence of the village.

The next day the sky was still dull and wet. It was not raining but in your skin and clothes you felt the cold of the water even if a breath of sirocco continued to blow from the Adriatic. The houses and gardens were dark down there from Casarsa along the Avenue of Remembrance to San Giovanni, San Floreano and along the long tree-lined road to the first little houses of Gruaro in the distance. Early in the morning when the sound of the matins bell had still not died away in the air and the old women had not yet come home from church to light the fire, the men and boys, and a few women too, began to gather at the workers' club in San Giovanni. With their wheels sunk in the mud, smelling of water and dung, five or six carts formed a line in the street in the cold shadows with the horses in the care of the youngest boys. Round about the members of the Young Pioneers — there were almost fifty of them with their bicycles — shouted impatiently, eager to leave for Rosa. 'What are we waiting for?' said Jacu. 'We'll never leave San Giovanni if we go along with these old men.'

'Gruaro won't go away!' shouted Eligio from the distance.

'The Pitottis and the other gentlemen can escape,' Jacu answered him. 'All we need to do, is speak to their foremen,' shouted Onorino with a laugh. 'Why don't you go,' Jacu said to him, 'and tell Susanna that we are going on ahead anyway.' 'It's best to keep together,' said Eligio uncertainly.

Meanwhile the rest, some astride their bicycles, others holding them by the handlebars, filled the street, talking loudly, calling to one another and shouting. They had fastened red ribbons in their buttonholes along with the Party badges. 'Who will we give the flag to?' said Eligio. 'Me,' shouted Onorino, who was standing next to him. 'Go on, let's give him it,' said Jacu. He ran into the empty Party rooms and took the flag.

When Onorino appeared at the door with the flag all the boys gathered round it with joyful cries and Onorino, in a state of excitement, began to wave it. 'Calm down, boys,' said Susanna. 'We're going on ahead,' said Eligio taking advantage of his good humour. 'That way,' he added, 'the others seeing that we youngsters are arriving at least won't start shouting if you are late.' 'Yes,' said Giovanni Blasut, 'maybe it's better if they go on meantime.' 'Off you go,' said Susanna then, 'but be careful on the road. No foolish business and great seriousness. Tell Leon we are coming right away.'

'We're off, boys,' shouted Eligio Pereisson. His brother Onorino with the flag and Livo went to the front and the group of youths set out through Borgo Braida towards San Florean and there, instead of taking the Guaro road, cut through the fields towards Madonna di Rosa by a side-road.

In front of the rain-washed ruins of the sanctuary and all over the main square there was already a big crowd waiting for the moment to set out for Gruaro. In the centre among the mingling groups, the cars and the bicycles, they could see Leon, with the leading Party members from Ligugnana and the most important branches, talking to the trade unionists who had come down from Udine and Pordenone. All round a group of young people from Ligugnana stood listening, looking at them with familiarity but with respect and keeping a certain distance. With one leg on the saddle of his bicycle, leaning one shoulder on the trunk of a chestnut-tree, Nini Infant was there with the others, calmly waiting for orders. Round his neck he had a long red scarf knotted two or three times under his chin.

'Nini!' Eligio shouted from the distance as they arrived in the centre of the square with the gang from San Giovanni. 'You old rascal,' shouted Nini, detaching himself from the chestnut-tree and pedalling to meet him. 'These are the boys from San Giovanni!' said Germano to Leon. 'Why are there so few of them?' the latter asked. 'It's only the young people,' said Germano. 'And the rest?' shouted Leon to the group which was coming closer. 'They'll be here soon,' shouted Eligio. 'Go and join the Pioneers from Ligugnana. You'll work with them,' said Leon and resumed his interrupted discussion with the other Party functionaries.

'Today, today!' shouted Nini.

'If I were in Count Spilimbergo's shoes I wouldn't be very happy,' said Eligio. Everyone was talking, shouting, looking for one another in the midst of the confusion; there was almost as big a crowd in the square of the Madonna di Rosa as on the day of the festival of the Madonna: hundreds of young people, almost all with red scarves round their necks, and older people on foot, crowded together, pushing and shoving, in the mud under the trees. The doors and windows of the houses were shut and beneath them, here and there, the flags of the Party branches showed red.

On Gruaro an almost blinding light fell from the overcast sky. Black and bare, the mountains of the Carnic Alps could be seen rising behind the station platform. But in the square, before the demonstrators – more than three thousand of them – had arrived from the direction of Madonna di Rosa and Prodolone it felt like an ordinary autumn day: in the bright light of the open air in the square between the two old Venetian gates the business of the morning went on as usual. The drivers from the Udine bus had gone into the big bar under the arcade to drink a coffee; a few old women went in and out of the church; girls went up and down on foot or on bicycles from the shops of the square to the fish-market. But almost in silence, as if they were scared, from Borgo Fontanis and Borgo Favria the demonstrators began to spread in long and disordered columns and in a quarter of an hour invaded the whole place.

Neither *carabinieri* nor police were to be seen in the square or in the streets. The people of Gruaro who had stayed outside showed no alarm and indeed some girls, returning home with their shopping-baskets full, shook their clenched fists at the houses of the rich, shouting: 'Put them to shame!' The demonstrators, as they gathered in the square, listened to them and laughed. In all the streets leading to the centre one could see groups of boys in overalls and red scarves or old partisan uniforms with camouflaged berets and the socks and boots taken from the Germans and the Americans. They sat on the kerbs or on the doorsteps and blocked entry. No longer could anyone enter or leave the centre of the village.

Under the arcades in front of the church the people from San

Giovanni had joined up with some of those from Ligugnana. Now it was beginning to drizzle from a sky which little by little had become dark.

'Where is Nini?' Eligio asked Basilio, who was riding quickly past. 'I'm going to find him,' said Eligio. 'No, you had better stay here with us,' said Onorino. 'Orders may arrive.' Eligio shrugged, 'I'll be back soon,' he said, taking his bicycle. 'We've got to be standing by,' Onorino insisted. But by now Eligio was riding away in the rain which was not heavy but rather like a thick mist. 'I'll be back soon,' he shouted. Under the arch of the gate a youth stopped him and asked him seriously: 'Where are you going? No one can go out.' But at that moment Nini appeared. 'Eligio!' he shouted, 'come here, my love.' The sentries at the gate had already procured two bottles of wine. 'Drink,' said Nini. With a laugh Eligio grabbed the neck and swallowed a couple of gulps.

'What are you doing?' Nini asked him. 'Nothing for the moment,' said Eligio. 'I feel like – ,' shouted Nini with a gesture as if he were throttling someone. 'Calm down,' said the boy who had stopped Eligio, 'didn't you hear the advice of Leon and the others from union headquarters? Don't go and mess things up by being stupid. We Communists are not thugs.' Nini shrugged but the argument was interrupted by Livo's voice calling Eligio from amid the crowd in the centre of the square. He kept making excited signs while Eligio took another swig at the bottle before leaving. Livo was scowling. 'The others are leaving,' he shouted. 'Get a move on, get a move on.' As soon as Eligio was close to him, Livo began to run in the direction of the fish-market instead of going off towards the arcades where they had been before. In the centre of the square hundreds of people were coming and going, laughing and cursing. 'Look at that, now we have lost them,' said Livo in a fury without looking at his brother. But at that moment someone from Ligugnana passed close by. 'Hey,' Livo shouted to him, 'have you seen our people – Susanna and the folk from San Giovanni?' 'They've gone down towards the Pitottis' villa,' the dark-haired boy answered with a threatening gesture. 'Keep going, comrades,' he added, shouting after the two brothers who had begun to run down the street leading to the schools. Behind them, on the other side of the moat which in past centuries surrounded the walls of Gruaro, the Pitottis' villa rose in the midst of a little garden. The garden and the road in front of it, along the brink of the moat, were all packed; the windows in the front of the house were shut. Livo and Eligio rejoined their group while Susanna, along with Giovanni Blasut and Jacu, were banging on the door. They had been banging for five minutes but no one came to open it.

'They're in there dying of fright,' said Livo.

'Hey, bosses, open up,' shouted Susanna, taking a couple of steps backwards on the gravel and looking towards the windows. 'Open up otherwise we'll break down the door.' After a minute or two the door opened and on the threshold a man of fifty appeared, fat, tall, bald — with a double-barrelled shotgun slung round his neck. It was Pitotti himself, one of the richest proprietors in the area. 'What do you want?' he asked.

'We want to talk to you,' said Susanna very loudly.

'There's about a hundred of you,' said Pitotti, 'I don't suppose you all want to come into my own house.'

'It only needs one person to talk,' said Susanna, still shouting.

'All right,' exclaimed Pitotti, 'but come in a proper deputation of at most four of you.'

After a few minutes of uncertainty Susanna, Blasut, Jacu and Eligio entered the corridor.

'This way,' said Pitotti.

He showed them into his office where there was a big desk, polished to a high pitch and shining like all the other pieces of furniture. The bookcases, which were reflected in the floor, were covered with files and dusty yellowing volumes. Behind the desk Pitotti's uncle was sitting; he too was tall and bald but his hands trembled either from age or fear. Pitotti went and stood behind the desk.

'Well, then,' he said. None of the workers had the courage to speak.

'I'm waiting for you to tell me what you want — if you would be so kind.' He spoke in the Venetian dialect of the mainland which is used by the middle classes in Friuli.

'You speak,' said Blasut in Friuli dialect to Susanna, who was the oldest.

Susanna began to speak, stammering and looking down. 'We have come,' he said, 'as we have and will continue to do . . . with all the agricultural workers of the zone so that . . . you will give work to the unemployed – that is your duty now that the de Gasperi measure has been passed.'

'The de Gasperi measure,' exclaimed Pitotti. 'There's been talk about it for months and I believe there has also been a ruling by the court in Udine.'

'A fine ruling! It has no validity for us,' answered Susanna, still looking at the ground, 'The representatives of the share-croppers withdrew before the ruling was given.'

'First of all, my dear fellow,' said Pitotti with sudden violence, 'good manners teach us that one should look a person in the face when talking.'

'Calm down, calm down, get off your high horse,' Eligio interrupted him decisively. 'You want to take advantage of ignoramuses like us because you have studied and are rich. No one taught us good manners.' He had a threatening air and his staring colourless eyes blazed.

'I meant,' said Pitotti, changing his tone, 'that it seemed as if he was looking for something on my floor. Are there rights squatting there too?'

'We have no right to your floor,' shouted Eligio. 'We have only the right to work.'

'And what can I do about it? I'm not the government.'

'Take on workers,' said Susanna. 'If all the landowners in the Gruara district each took in a small number of unemployed here, too, the de Gasperi measure would be applied peacefully.'

'I've told you there's a ruling by the court at Udine. I stand by that.'

'That ruling was wrong. Why should the measure apply only to a fifth of Friuli? All right, no one says anything and at Cervignano, at Nimis and in the flooded districts of the plain maybe there will be more misery than here. But have we to die of hunger because of that?'

'I've told you I've got nothing to do with it. I am a private citizen like you – I have my family and I work for them.'

'You eat every day,' said Eligio. 'But there are some people who when they get up in the morning don't know if they will eat or not before they go to bed.'

Pitotti spread his arms. 'So you don't give that a thought?' said

Eligio. 'You don't give it a thought. Then who should?'

'Our employers' federation,' said Pitotti, 'made proposals that come some way to meet you.'

'Great proposals! And then these proposals, you began to make them after weeks of agitation, but for that you'd never have thought, would you, of saying to these poor people: "Look, here's a plate of minestra, eat, you dog?" '

'Well, we did what we could.'

'Oh no, by taking on a hundred and twenty unemployed you only get to a figure of four per cent of the agricultural increment. The union was right not to accept it. In all the Gruara area to give work to six hundred unemployed — it's not a great deal that we demand.'

'These are all excuses,' Pitotti suddenly shouted in a rage. 'All excuses to conceal the political background of your demonstrations.'

'Political background!' replied Eligio growing red. 'There are people out of work and if you don't believe me come with me and I'll take you to their houses to see what poverty is. There you can be sure you won't find marble floors,' he added, stamping on the ground.

'To sum up,' Pitotti interrupted him, 'you would like me like that, on my own initiative, to begin to take on workers. I tell you right away I won't do it! I cannot go against the law nor even against the guideline of my federation.'

'But if you have a little heart you won't worry about the court or the federation. By taking on workers you help families who are dying of poverty.'

'I understand,' said Pitotti, 'but I can't on my own go against all my own colleagues.' So saying he had made to go towards the corridor.

'Is that your last word?' said Susanna, looking a little pale, and shifting his cap on his head.

'Yes.'

The four men did not move, not knowing what they should do.

'But not ours!' shouted Jacu suddenly. 'Let's go, comrades.' He left the office quickly together with the others. When they reached the garden door the hundred or so demonstrators who

61

stood waiting for the result of the discussion crowded round the delegates in the doorway.

'He doesn't agree! He doesn't agree!' shouted Jacu.

'Give him a hiding, you'll see he'll agree,' cried one of the crowd. 'Keep calm, comrades,' shouted Susanna. But by now, they were excited. Everyone was pushing towards the entrance, shaking their fists. 'What do they want?' asked Pitotti, who had followed the four to the door. 'To kill you,' Jacu shouted at him in Friuli dialect. Susanna managed to make the men be quiet for a moment. 'All right,' he said, 'if we have to occupy this house, let's occupy it. We'll all go in now. But watch what you do, comrades. I'll send for Leon and he will come and do the talking.'

'Come in, comrades,' shouted Eligio. Everyone rushed into the corridor and crowded together there right up to the big staircase that led to the upper storeys. The boys sat against the walls on the floor and began to smoke. Susanna, Eligio, Jacu and Blasut went into the office with Pitotti and sat on the desk. They had sent Livo to call Leon. 'But who'll be able to find Leon now?' said Susanna. 'He can't be in a hundred places at once like St Anthony!' Meantime the house echoed with the shouts, the laughter and the discussions of the workers. A little group of four or five had gone to sit on the stairs under the marble railing; and after twenty minutes or so, since everyone was getting tired, they struck up a song. They passed almost an hour like this, singing, while outside the rain stopped and at midday the air cleared. 'He's coming right away!' shouted Livo, entering the office in a sweat. And in fact a few minutes later Leon arrived with two officials from the union headquarters. He was a man of thirty, tall with huge shoulders; he had a white, square face with a hooked nose, drooping moustaches and eyes that were bleak and determined.

He entered the villa hurriedly and everyone gathered round him, greeting him with assurance. 'Where is Susanna?' Leon asked shortly. Then in a few words Susanna told how things had gone. 'Bring him here,' said Leon. Susanna went to get Pitotti from the office.

After quarter of an hour's discussion Pitotti stated that he would sign an agreement in which he promised to take on workers.

By now the midday bells were ringing. It looked as if it were turning fine again; the tired, harsh light spread over the walls and roofs of the town which, behind the moat, stretched darkly round the sports field. Following Leon, who was talking to the out-of-town functionaries, the group passed back across the bridge and into town towards the square. With the brighter light and the sound of the bells there was an almost festive air. Torrents of demonstrators crossed the square; others were sitting in the arcades; on the towers, here and there, there were still sentries. They had nothing to do and leant against the walls, chatting among themselves or shouting to their comrades passing through the square. The moment he arrived back Eligio ran straight away to Nini who was sitting on the ground in the wet with his blood-red scarf which he had wrapped round his neck. 'San Giovanni,' he shouted, 'have a drink!' and held out the bottle to Eligio.

'Anyone who hasn't had orders to stay in Gruaro,' shouted Basilio as he arrived on his bicycle, 'Leon said can go home to eat.'

Nini and the others of the guard did not move and listened to Basilio with a lack of interest.

'Are you staying here?' Eligio asked Nini.

'Yes, we on the gate are staying,' said Nini.

'And what are you going to eat?'

'The women from Ligugnana are bringing us food.'

But at that moment a voice called them: 'Hey, comrades.' It was Milio, white and red, with his eyes as hard as glass and deepest blue. He looked at them and laughed.

'Milio! Where have you popped out from?' Nini shouted to him also laughing.

'Where do you think! I'm here too, like you.'

'Have a drink,' Nini shouted to him.

'Yes, I'll have a drink. I've such a hangover I can hardly see,' said Milio, and suddenly with good spirits added: 'I'm going to eat something at my uncle's – near here. Why don't you come with me?'

'We'll come, damn it!' said Nini. 'Come on, Eligio.'

And he followed Milio with Eligio at his back whereas the others went off in the opposite direction. Onorino had taken up his flag again and waved it about at the head of the group which followed him, singing.

VII

The cottage of Milio's uncle and aunt, the Faedis, was half-way between Gruaro and Rosa, in the middle of the countryside.

Immediately behind it the shallows of the Tagliamento began and farther back still the hollow of the shingle-bed of the river, as big as a lake under the shadows of the mountains.

A little sun had come out and the three friends pedalled gaily along the country road with the hedges on either side half stripped by the autumn, dripping with rain.

The first thing they saw at the end of a strip of land between the vines – there beside the muddy road among the tangled rows – was an amazingly pale little girl with a huge tress of hair, which she was incapable of keeping upright, so thin and tiny was she. She had huge lamb's eyes – they really did go with the mass of hair – but which apparently could see nothing, just like those of a new-born lamb.

Yet she must have been sixteen or seventeen. Near her was another girl, younger in age but much less shy who, unlike the other, stared fixedly at the three mates as they arrived cheerful and mud-splashed.

'Ciao, Cecilia, ciao Ilde,' said Milio. 'Aren't you going to say hello?'

Ilde, the smaller one, at least said a very faint 'Ciao'. But Cecilia only lowered her eyes and bent her head as if the great tress of hair had won and had managed to bend her double.

But the three friends, for their part, did not even look at her. They paid no attention to that sucking calf there, with her feet in the wet grass among the vines, standing and wondering goodness knows what. They rode quickly into the Faedis' courtyard through the gate which was half eaten away by the rains. And there once more Milio shouted a greeting: 'Salve, cousins!'

They were two little boys washing a horse at the trough.

'Hey, Nisiuti,' said Milio laughing, 'you're always there with that horse – you'd be better off with a girlfriend!'

The smaller boy, with a quiff of hair over his forehead, looked at him and laughed, standing there firmly with his legs wide apart in white stockings. 'Eh, of course,' he said. But the bigger one, who was called Nesto, said: 'Now you'll hear what my father has to say. Goodness knows what he'll give you for going to the square like a fool.'

'What can he say to me?' said Milio shrugging. 'I've acted in his interest to, not just in our own!'

'Yes, yes,' Nesto replied, currying Marco, the colt, very hard, 'but not the interest of the parish priest.'

'Good boy,' said Nini, leaning his bicycle against the stone wall along with Eligio. 'After supper you'll come to the square with us, eh? And we'll set fire to the parish priest's bum!'

All the Faedis were inside the house in the big kitchen with its hearth. They were not the kind of people who went about causing trouble, for this reason or that, with hammer or sickle. 'We were born poor and poor we will die,' the father of Nesto and Nisiuti always said – old Erminio Faedis, who was the head of the family.

Now he was there with one foot on the hearthstone lighting his pipe, poking among the embers that gave little explosions in the heap of firewood.

'Ciao uncle, good day to all,' said Milio as he came in with that higher and sharper voice he had when he was merry or when he was a little embarrassed.

'These are my two comrades,' he said then. 'There'll be a bit of bread and cheese for them!' he added, always good-humoured.

'Sit down, sit down,' said old Anuta, who was also by the hearth.

'Who are they?' said old Faedis, spitting with unheard of violence and pulling furiously on his pipe.

'This is Nini Infant from Ligugnana and this is Eligio Pereisson from San Giovanni,' said Milio.

66

Old Faedis's younger brother, Francesco, who was a little man with no teeth but with a face full of goodness and gentleness, said to Eligio: 'I'm a friend of your father's, we did military service together. Ah, we're old mates!'

Eligio and Nini sat down on the edge of the straw-bottomed chairs round the big table in the centre of the kitchen.

'Yes, he's told me,' said Eligio.

'How many of you are there?' asked Francesco.

'There's me, two smaller brothers and my sister Alba,' said Eligio.

'Then your father's done better than me,' said Francesco, opening wide his toothless mouth. 'He's had four children and I've only got three: two girls, the ones you saw outside – the two mad ones – and this one here.' And he pointed at a little boy of two or three, bundled up in his rags, who was playing with a puppy on the floor.

'My father's a jackass,' said Eligio. 'The fewer mouths there are the better off you are.'

Everyone laughed – old Anuta, Francesca, the younger wives – and especially the daughters, the ones Nini had really been looking at from the moment he entered. Now there they were laughing, as fresh and firm as statues, with a lot of frizzy hair about their round cheeks. The prettiest was a girl called Regina, eldest daughter of the oldest of the Faedis clan.

'But I think I know you,' said Nini looking at her.

'Maybe,' said Regina, blushing like a glowing ember, because all eyes were on her.

'But aren't you the girlfriend of Ernesto Castellarin, the one that works at the Mangiarotti factory?'

'Yes,' said Regina, blushing even more.

'He's a friend of mine,' said Nini. 'He's lucky,' he added, 'he's got a good job.'

'Of course he has a good job,' said old Faedis, clearing his throat. 'If not, I wouldn't have given him my daughter!'

'That's what I meant,' Nini commented, 'if you're a friend of the priest you get the best jobs and the rest can go you know where.'

Old Faedis look at him angrily: 'Aren't you a friend of his? That means you're a friend of the priest too.'

'I'm everybody's friend,' said Nini, 'but no one will make me change my ideas.'

'Great!' said old Erminio, who was red-haired and got angry easily.

But at that moment a shrill voice, one fit to damage one's ears, was heard shrieking from the courtyard.

'Folks!' shouted the woman's voice.

'Ah, it's the Owl,' said Anuta, as if she knew her of old, and along with the rest she prepared for the visit.

Sure enough the Owl, a young married woman, entered immediately, all white and red, bursting out of her clothes and her hair, which was tightly drawn back.

'Oooh,' she said the moment she entered, putting a hand in front of her mouth. She had seen that there were guests and now she fell silent, exaggerating her surprise and embarrassment.

It was just what was needed to avert a discussion that could have become somewhat unpleasant. At Rosa everyone knew that the Faedis were in with the priest while Nini, who was from Ligugnana, could not know.

Everyone looked at the Owl with laughter in their eyes as she stood there with a hand in front of her mouth and in the other a bottle for oil.

'Speak up,' said old Anuta protectively.

'I've got no oil left,' said the Owl in embarrassment, 'and I had come to see if you could lend me some.'

'Yes, yes,' said Anuta, 'come here.'

And Regina, trying to be funny, said a bit cheekily: 'So long as you let us have it back!'

'My name's not Regina!' said the Owl with her head high and her Adam's apple much in evidence, referring to something that had happened — goodness knows when and goodness knows why — between her and these women but which at this moment seemed to be entirely to her advantage.

'Silly girl, silly girl,' said Anuta to her as, stooping a little, she poured out the oil. And everyone laughed, their faces looking as if a flame of merriment had burnt them red.

The one to stir the polenta was Francesco's wife and Erminio's sister-in-law — Giuditta, a woman almost as ruddy in the face as the Owl, although older, with thick lips and little eyes swollen with laughter. She finished by giving the last stir to the pot with the stick and poured out the polenta.

'Come on, call them all in, it's ready!' she shouted as she bustled about. Regina went to the door that gave on to the courtyard and began to shout like a lost soul: 'Nesto! Nisiuti! Ceciliaaa!'

Nesto and Nisiuti were there having run from the stable where they had put the colt, Marco, shining all over like gold, but Cecilia and Ilde these two —

'Ceciliaaa!' Regina kept on shouting.

Ah yes! As if these two would come. Regina's voice lost itself without avail in the courtyard with all its gear, beyond the midden, beyond the apple orchard, beyond the fields with all the files of vines which stood almost naked among the black mulberries, far, far away in the peace of the midday fields.

The only voice that replied to Regina's was that of the bells of Rosa borne along by a warmish wind from the sea that shook the tops of the poplars in the distance and the greenish tendrils of the vines close by.

'That one won't come even if we kill her!' said Francesco with a slightly embarrassed smile on his toothless cat's mouth.

'Why?' asked Eligio. 'What's she afraid of?'

'Of you, because you're young men!' said Nesto quickly; he, too, had had that special smile which the Faedis apparently always gave when Cecilia's shyness came up.

'We won't eat her!' said Nini, who felt a slight confusion at the thought of that pretty, timid little lass.

The smallest brother, Nisiuti, put on a mischievous look and said: 'If you tell her she's engaged she begins to cry from shame.'

'You keep quiet, you still piss the bed,' said his mother, shutting him up. But he was not in the least put out and sitting at his plate said like a man: 'Isn't it ready yet?'

After a while they all began to eat polenta and sausage which smelt good enough to bring the dead back to life. The Owl stood there with her oil-bottle in her hand, prolonging the visit because it was too interesting to leave. And it was a good idea, for Erminio sent Nesto three or four times to draw wine in the cellar and in half an hour they were all half-drunk, especially the women, who were less used to drinking than the men.

69

They all had the giggles but were not so drunk as not to notice, and to hide it, they made awkward and naïve gestures, cleaning their grimy hands on the tablecloth and raising their arms to the sky to call on the Lord, with the result that they became more and more embarrassed and rediscovered in certain folds of their wrinkled skin the blushing red of young brides.

The youths, too, were amused at the merriment of their elders and teased them.

'Who knows how they'll laugh behind our backs,' said Anuta, red in the face.

Nini and Eligio, who were at the centre of the merriment, reassured her: 'No, no, signora, why should we laugh?'

'They'll say you are old fools!' shouted Regina from beside the hearth; she had finished eating and was there with the other girls, all with their faces fiery red.

'You keep quiet, you stupid thing!' said her mother. The girl covered her face with her arm, laughing, and another, still younger, defended her: 'We have the right to say our say too!'

'First of all try to find some idiot to marry you and when you are mistress of your own house you'll be able to say anything that comes into your mind.'

'Well, maybe even now we say fewer silly things than you.'

'They give themselves airs because they read that magazine, *Grand Hotel*!' said Nesso mockingly.

'That's it! The boy's right,' shouted Giuditta, Francesco's wife, 'he's got more common sense than the two of you together!'

Then Milio jumped up. The wine had tinged his porcelain-white skin pink and made his blue eyes dart here and there.

'What are you saying?' he exclaimed, running over to the hearth and, catching a girl under the chin, forced her to turn round and show herself to everyone. 'What are you saying?' he repeated. 'You're old, auntie, and you come out with your wisdom. But what do you expect them to know about wisdom with these two faces made for kissing?'

The girl wriggled free and threatened him with the broom which was leaning there against the wall of the hearth. And the old woman shouted angrily: 'Leave my daughter alone, God – '

'Damn it,' Nesto finished off.

'Listen to him,' exclaimed old Anuta, 'just like his cousin.'

The rascally cousin meanwhile took the broom with which he had been threatened and threw it into Eligio's arms, making it sail right across the kitchen. 'Here, sing!' he shouted.

Eligio caught the broom in mid-flight, crouched on his chair holding the broom in his arms like a guitar and began to sing the song he sang when he was drinking:

'*Dia bredar, then darling squer, bredar, iu nou mai ert, tuingling then . . .*'

He was deathly pale with white skin under the blond quiff that fell over his eyes like a rag and his blue eyes ringed with red. He hadn't been well since he came back from Yugoslavia.

'Go and draw some more wine,' Erminio ordered his nephew Nesto, who ran off at once.

'Oh don't bother for us!' said Nini, while round about everybody was laughing to hear Eligio's songs accompanied on the broom.

'We may be poor but a glass of wine!' exclaimed Anuta, barely touching the words with her tongue as if they were explosive charges, so as to seem as well brought up as possible, and the others, hearing her talk so grandly, could not keep in their laughter.

'Stupid things!' said the old woman, abashed, and laughed herself. The men drank while the women, against their wills, pretended they didn't want any more.

'You put on this fuss just so that we'll look at you,' said Francesco, the angel, with his little toothless mouth.

'And then when we're not here they go down to the cellar and drink in secret!' added Erminio Faedis, with his redhead's voice.

'Poor old things!' said the women, half under their breath and laughed. It looked as if the two men paid less attention to the guests than the women but clearly Erminio had been thinking about them all the time. Indeed he turned to Nini, lit his pipe, and said: 'In big peasant families things never go well — someone's always shouting, another's crying, another's arguing — it's a — a — ' He sought for a word, for a simile, but although he spoke better than the women his assurance had left him.

'Brothel,' Milio concluded from behind the hearth. The girls gave a cry.

'You should be ashamed,' they shouted. And the Owl, who

71

was half out of breath from speaking and passing remarks, sang to cover things up:

You can't always be merry
Nor always sa-a-a-d . . .

Milio turned to the old man, and asked unabashed: 'Isn't that what you meant?'

The old man muttered something, taking the first puffs at his pipe, which he had finally succeeded in lighting, threw into the hearth the twig he had used, and went on with his speech: 'Here there are sixteen of us and each one wants to assert his rights. One needs a dress, another needs injections, one wants this and another wants that. And we poor men, woe betide us if we don't see to everything, if we don't always have our eyes open,' and he made an awkward gesture, clasping the pipe in his hands and opening his eyes wide. Leaning forward, he nearly fell to the ground.

'Big families,' he went on addressing the guests with a confidential air, 'should split up. Each one for himself! But how can we? Look at this! Two girls with their lips still sticky with milk.'

'Oh Lord!' shouted the girls, raising their arms to heaven.

'A whole row of calves that haven't finished elementary school. Nesto, there — in the shop. And then who works the land? We have to stay together — there's no other way.'

Then Nini who had sat there silently with a black lock falling over his face, which the wine had made pale, shouted: 'Ah, boss, how do you have the courage to complain when you've all that land!'

While Nini was speaking the door opened very quietly and Cecilia came in and stood there looking at him.

No one had noticed her because they were all caught up in the discussion. And least of all Nini.

'Yes, look here!' said the old man quickly, 'how many mouths to feed.'

'When there's enough to give them, that's fine. What's bad is if the necessary's lacking,' said Nini.

'I'm not saying that,' muttered the old man. 'Thank heaven we don't lack bread.'

'Or wine!' shouted Milio.

'And rouge for the girls!' Nesto wanted to add.

'Listen to these two damned cousins!' old Anuta intervened.

'Speak properly,' the head of the family hurled at her.

'Ignorant and foul-mouthed we were born and so we shall die!' Anuta countered.

'And you complain,' Nini continued, 'but what am I to say then, a poor labourer who hasn't even a square metre of earth of my own? Working all year to have never a copper in my pocket.'

'We are born to work and wear ourselves out, there's no use having any other idea in your head!' With Nini the old man was rather severe and to continue now turned more to Eligio.

'Look,' he said almost as if on purpose, 'if here in this family there wasn't a little religion to keep us together – to make us know our duty and resign ourselves to it – '

'Resign yourselves to what?' Nini interrupted him. His eyes were shining in his dark face and round his neck, tightly tied, was the red scarf which made him look almost like a bandit.

Cecilia watched him from her corner and almost began to cry under her great tress of hair for fear that hard words would be exchanged between him and her older uncle.

'Resign yourselves!' Nini repeated darkly. 'Maybe you lack for nothing – you have a full granary and cellar, with all that wine you can buy yourself a dress for the fair each year, all of you, and put something aside as well, and I know that you are Church people and if someone lets out an oath like Anuta did just then, you are scandalized!'

He spoke jokingly but with a certain forced sincerity and with anger behind his gaze.

Once again to scupper the argument, the Owl, from the corner near the hearth, opened her mouth and with all the breath in her body – and she had plenty – began to sing deafeningly: 'You can't always be merry, nor always sa-a-a-d.'

And Eligio took up the broom again, standing this time with his feet apart and firmly set on the tiled floor, and began to sing in English in a boogie-woogie rhythm: 'Then then blin fadr farar, bounding – '

To that rhythm Milio took the Owl by the hips and forced her to dance, making her spin like a top on the floor although she protested, screeching like an eagle.

73

Everyone began to laugh as before, their faces burning with merriment and their mouths open, leaning forward from the waist, the children more loudly than the grown-ups, taking advantage of their good humour, and the grown-ups louder than the children, enjoying this moment of respite from their thoughts and cares.

Even the last two to come in – the two wild ones – laughed, Cecilia and Ilde, laughed, poor things. Cecilia almost had tears in her lamb's eyes, but she too laughed with the others, laughed and laughed.

Then the three young men left. That little bit of sun which had peeped out at midday through the clouds had disappeared once more and it was black all round. But not in the boys' hearts.

They pedalled towards Gruaro at full speed, singing.

Gruaro was full of people all ready for the fight; no one had ever seen so many young people all together. It was as if, three or four years earlier, all the partisans had come down from the mountains.

They were all in the square round the villa of the Spilimbergos, who were neither Pitottis nor Malacarts. They were a tough bone to pick, the Counts. There was no one at home; this lot lived almost all the time in Rome. First of all Leon and the other leading members were patient, telephoning to the overseers here and there, then they gave the 'all clear' to their men. In the twinkling of an eye the demonstrators threw down the gate and entered the villa, which was a palace.

Nini, Milio, Eligio, Jacu and the younger ones went and sat on the velvet armchairs.

Then, satisfied, they went into the cellars: down there it was wine and sausages. Lots of people carried sacks of sugar and flour for which their poor mothers in Ligugnana and Rosa blessed them.

But just when things were at their height, squads of police arrived from Pordenone with an armoured car. The boys of the Pioneers inside the villa from being besiegers became besieged. But there was nothing that could be done that day against the power of the people. When the armoured car knocked down the surrounding wall and went into the garden with the police on top pointing their weapons, suddenly a woman – then two, then three, then a hundred – went and lay down on the ground in the mud and the pouring rain. And there they stayed – and who could move them? – shouting to the police: 'Go on, go on, if you have the courage, sons of dogs!'

So the police, a few at a time, had to go back where they came from and, towards evening, a telephone call came as well from the Spilimbergos' administrator saying he accepted the demonstrators' conditions.

Nini and the others were in the villa when the news arrived: 'The administrator has accepted the conditions which the other landowners have already accepted!' Jacu, who was dead drunk, threw the string of sausages he had seized into the air, and began to kick the empty bottles. 'Come out, come out, comrades!' shouted Susanna. 'We have won!'

It was dark by now and you could see the shadows of the defeated police and soldiers beyond the archways of the gates. A large part of the crowd had already poured out of the garden into the square, filling it with noise and shouts and singing. Here and there the lights began to come on in the windows of the houses, not in the square but in the quarters round about beyond the moat. Everyone was shouting to the others, exchanging greetings joyfully.

In a corner Onorino, still with his flag, was astride his bicycle on the gleaming mud along with the others from San Giovanni. 'Tomorrow it's San Giovanni's turn!' said Nini as he said goodbye to Eligio and the rest. 'Tomorrow,' Jacu shouted grimly, 'we'll show the gentlemen!' 'Till tomorrow then,' said Nini. 'Come on, Infant,' shouted his companions who were setting out for Ligugnana. 'Till tomorrow,' Eligio shouted after him. Then each one pedalled light-heartedly home because of the famous victory.

VIII

A sad dark morning descended on San Giovanni. On the mud and puddles of the previous day, which had remained during the hours of sleep, the sky, covered by low white clouds, as motionless as the mud and the puddles, glowed without light. Against its gleams the walls of smoky stone and the roofs of San Giovanni stood out darkly, soaking wet, in a silence which the occasional crowing of the cocks from the courtyards of Braida or Romans made more cheerless.

Although usually, at the sound of the matins bell ringing across the still dark village, scarcely touched by the first pink of dawn, life began very early, that morning the state of nocturnal withdrawal seemed still to lie heavy on the clusters of houses, even although the day was already fairly far advanced. On the main street of San Giovanni, sunk in a light which did not go so far as to illuminate it, shutters and outside doors were closed. In the clusters of houses towards the fields the women, just back from morning service, were giving grain to the birds or lighting the fire, doing their daily tasks in silence and in haste, as on some sad occasions such as a death or a misfortune in the family. In front of the workers' club all the Communists, the labourers, the unemployed, were gathered almost in silence awaiting the arrival of the people from the neighbouring villages and almost trembling in the icy air of dawn.

Only towards eight did the groups from Ligugnana arrive on their bicycles; but there were not more than two hundred of them. They put their bicycles in the courtyard of the club. With them San Giovanni woke up a little; since they weren't in their own village they shouted and sang without fear. 'By midday it will be all over at San Giovanni,' said Nini to Eligio. 'You don't know Malacart,' Eligio replied. 'He's a bastard.' They had gone into the workers' club, which was untidy from the previous evening with splashes of wine and mud and the flag leaning against the bar. Jacu was there, still drunk from the previous night, with his elbows on the bar in front of a glass of grappa, with his face as gaunt as a consumptive's and his eyes almost unfocused although they were set in a threatening stare. Round about were Susanna and the others; they were worried because, apart from Ligugnana, those from the nearby villages were not arriving; and those from Ligugnana were fewer than half of what had been agreed.

'Things will go badly today,' said Susanna.

'Badly,' shouted Jacu, 'who for?' and he began to laugh.

'Don't get upset, master,' said Nini to Susanna, who was a carpenter by trade. 'We'll see to it.'

'What do you think?' replied Susanna. 'That the police have gone back to Pordenone, to Padua or to Mestre?'

'Never mind where they've gone,' shouted Nini with a shrug, 'we couldn't care less.'

'Yesterday,' said Jacu, 'it was the women of Gruaro who did the job. But if they come back today we'll deal with them.'

From the road to Pordenone singing could be heard. 'There they are!' said Susanna, going to the door. In the air, which seemed to grow darker as the day went on, the songs coming from the direction of Pordenone had a discordant echo which was not cheering. Shortly afterwards the demonstrators from Prodolone, Savorgnano, Cannedo and the other parishes appeared.

'All here?' said Susanna, seeing that they too were no more numerous than the people from Ligugnana. But they were in good spirits and stopped in front of the workers' club; before putting their bicycles inside they wanted to finish up by singing the Internationale at the top of their voices.

'They're sleeping in San Giovanni!' shouted a youth from Cannedo. 'Yes, sleeping,' said Eligio, 'if only they could.' The newcomers caused a great stir, shouting and calling to one another in front of the club as they laid down their bicycles. 'Only the people from Gruaro are missing,' said Susanna. 'They have an easy life – they're not peasants.' 'But the peasants of San Giovanni are having a holiday too today,' said one of the men from Ligugnana. 'Yes, they're all sitting shut up in their houses,' said another. 'And where are we from?' said Onorino. 'We're talking about the bosses,' said the man from Ligugnana, 'and those silly bastards who are on their side.'

Shortly afterwards the people from Gruaro arrived too; they split into three columns and spread through the town.

The Malacarts' house was half-way between the club and the square, near the school; it too stood in the middle of a garden surrounded by a high wall. At the end of this wall was the square with the church and the co-operative store and immediately beyond that the arcades. There, in the square and in the centre, everything was enclosed in silence, as if uninhabited, until the demonstrators left the club. Singing, with red scarves round their necks, they arrived in an irregular column before the church where the light was so poor that it looked as if it was going to start raining again at any minute. In the village, however, there was basically a sense of tranquillity and almost of absorption in which the footsteps, the voices, the singing of the striking workers seemed to sink, to have a fleeting significance by which the ancient peace of San Giovanni was scarcely impaired.

But in less than a quarter of an hour shouts and whistles were heard echoing confusedly from time to time from the direction of the Malacart villa. As in Gruaro the day before, the workers were occupying the house. The largest group packed the streets between the schools and the square. There, too, the gate of the villa, which gave on to the bare and dripping garden, was shut and beyond you could see the house, which appeared to be uninhabited. The workers began to beat on the gate and to throw stones into the garden beyond the wall. Some stones even reached the front of the house, striking the doors and windows or a tin roof; but in the house everything remained shut and silent. The demonstrators in the street shouted and whistled. After a while they began to hammer at the lock of the gate with an iron bar. At these blows, which were more violent and determined than the others, the head of a man with red hair and a complexion of almost the same colour appeared.

'What do you want?' he yelled.

'We want to speak to you.'

'Speak!' he said still yelling. 'What about?'

'Open up,' they shouted from the street. 'If not we'll knock down the gate and all come into your house.'

'Criminals!' he yelled and closed the shutters again.

The others started taking the gate off its hinges again but shortly Malacart appeared in the door with a shotgun in his hands. 'Let's hear what you have to say,' he shouted. 'One of you come forward.'

From behind him the old serving-woman came out of the half-open door and, limping across the courtyard to the gate, opened it. 'If more than one comes in, I'll fire,' he shouted.

The demonstrators discussed among themselves for a few minutes, then Susanna walked with the old woman towards the door. He stayed inside for more than half an hour. Meanwhile it began to rain again. The demonstrators crowded in long lines against the walls of the houses opposite under the gutters and in the doorways. A few went as far as the arcade and under the porch of the church almost two hundred metres from the villa. The rain spattered hard on the mud and the puddles. At last Susanna came out into the garden, pushing his beret back above his red, burnt face, as if he had been drinking. He was laughing as he walked forward with his hands in his pockets.

'No go, no go!' he said.

Everyone ran round him. 'How was it?' shouted those further away.

'Nothing, he doesn't want to,' the others replied angrily, both indignant and discouraged. In a few moments almost everyone had crowded in front of the gate shouting.

'Come on, let's go in,' shouted Blasut.

'Let's go in, it's his fault,' said Susanna. They took a few steps into the garden to occupy it but a shutter opened on the ground floor and the barrel of the shotgun poked out.

They scattered behind the wall on either side of the gate and began to throw stones at the villa without taking aim. They could hear the stones hitting the walls or the tin roof of the wood-store.

Jacu, who had gone with Eligio and the other comrades to shelter from the rain under the arcade, came and asked Susanna what had happened.

'The old robber,' said Susanna, 'he doesn't want to meet our claims.'

'He'd sell his mother for a hundred lire, that one,' shouted Eligio.

'At Ligugnana,' said Nini, 'we'd have settled matters by now.'

'What shall we do?' Jacu asked Susanna, looking him in the eye. Susanna shrugged. 'For the present we're keeping him shut up in his house,' he said. 'He'll have to make up his mind. He's tough but we're tougher.'

Jacu continued to look hard at him; and the rain had made his hair stick to his brow and over his eyes. 'I'll do something about it, damn it,' he shouted and walked forward pushing the half-open gate wide. They could still see the barrel poking from behind the shutter. Before Susanna, who had followed him, could stop him, he pulled his pistol from his jacket pocket and fired a shot at the window. An instant later the shotgun replied. The bullet ended up a few metres above the heads of some men who were standing in a line under the gutter against the wall of a cottage.

Jacu raised his arm to fire from behind the gate-pillar but Susanna seized him by the sleeve. 'Don't fire,' he shouted. 'That's enough.'

'Stop,' Eligio said to him, 'you're mad.'

'But he deserves it, the bastard,' shouted Nini.

'They'd all deserve it,' said Blasut, 'but meantime we'll still get better terms.'

'Leave me,' said Jacu, white in the face and almost trembling. 'Leave me, damn it, I want to show that son of a bitch.'

'I'm going in,' said Onorino Pereisson suddenly. 'I want to see if he has the guts to fire.'

'Listen to him,' said Susanna. 'Get away from here, baby-face. I don't want trouble from your father.'

'My father won't do anything to you,' said the boy.

'He won't do anything,' shouted Susanna, 'because you're not moving from here.'

'Come on, let me go in, he hasn't got it in him to shoot.'

Livo, who was there next to Onorino in his short trousers and Chini, another of their mates, who wasn't more than fifteen, said: 'We're going with Onorino.'

'At Gruaro it was the women,' shouted Onorino, 'and today it's us — the baby-faces.'

He pulled himself free from Susanna and, followed by his two companions, went through the gate and began to walk up the path.

A shot rang out, but Malacart had fired in the air just to frighten them.

'Boss, boss!' shouted Susanna, sticking his head out, 'watch what you're doing, they're boys.'

But behind the boys, who continued to advance very slowly, the bolder ones followed almost in silence.

'Watch out,' said Susanna, 'that one's got no pity.'

Little by little they invaded the whole garden and the foremost had reached the door when someone came running from the direction of Gruaro and shouted that the police were arriving from the main road.

Before all the workers had left Malacart's garden, at the end of the street through Borgo Braida, between the windowless stone houses, the armoured car of the previous day could be seen approaching, followed by three or four trucks packed with police. The column had stopped almost opposite the workers' club and slowly, grasping their weapons firmly, the men were jumping down from the trucks into the mud of the street. Susanna sent a boy to call the people who had gone off towards Casarsa.

'We're not moving from here,' he said. 'If they begin hitting, we'll hit back.'

Almost everyone had a stick or a bill-hook and, standing close together, formed a kind of barricade in the middle of the street. The armoured car, which was open, advanced slowly towards them. 'Disperse,' the captain shouted standing up on his seat. No one replied. He shouted the order two or three times. The armoured car was only a few metres from the workers, continuing to advance at walking pace without stopping until it was up against the people in front. They gave way, crowding to the right and left of the street. The armoured car continued until it had gone right through the crowd, but when the police behind it tried to follow, the demonstrators barred their way. The police threatened them, shaking their truncheons and the crowd raised their bill-hooks, sticks and fists. At that moment, the people who at the arrival of the troops had scattered among the gardens and fields appeared, walking in a disorderly way and shouting; at almost the same moment those whom Susanna had called arrived from the square. The police, seeing such a throng arriving from all sides and closing round the armoured car, became alarmed and began hitting out. In a few minutes in the middle of the street there was nothing but a mass of bodies, locked in a confused fight.

The whole street from the schools to the square was in an uproar and no one could make out what was happening anywhere else. There were three or four hundred workers but there were a lot of police too. The fight was most bitter in front of Malacart's gate and from there it spread in all directions.

But the older men began to detach themselves and merely fended off the police when they attacked and pushed them. They looked at them in the same sort of way as children look at grown-ups when they tell them off, shutting themselves away behind a look that was partly one of caution, partly of hatred. They turned their humiliation into a kind of postponement until more propitious times – a repressed threat. They went off alone or in groups from the centre of the fighting, slowly, as if they didn't want it to be noticed. Some took shelter along the walls of the houses; others made their way along the cliff-like walls of the enormous Gothic church, built fifty years before, and along the little street which led between the church and the arcade to the sacristy and the priests' cinema. And from there they stood and watched what was happening in the mud in the middle of the square. Others had even turned off into Borgo Romans and removed themselves a score of metres from the square.

It was above all those from San Giovanni, who lived round about, that gave way and withdrew. The boys from the other villages however, especially Ligugnana, continued to stand there round the armoured car, fighting in a ragged way with the police, mixing their blows with arguments and insults. But they had the worse of it because they did not feel sure of what they were doing, feeling isolated and left to themselves. Many of them with bruises and some of them bleeding followed the older men from San Giovanni down through Borgo Romans and went into the houses to bathe their wounds.

But suddenly there appeared, coming down the Avenue of Remembrance from Casarsa, four or five army trucks full of soldiers. They stopped at the corner of the square under the red wall of the Sanctuary. When Susanna who, while not taking part in the boys' exchange of blows, was with them, along with Blasut and some other older members of the branch, saw them, he pushed his cap back on his head and said to those around him: 'Let's go, let's go' and made off towards Borgo Romans, followed by the others.

'Let's go, let's go,' he kept on saying as he passed through those who all around were continuing the skirmish with the police.

'Not all in the same direction,' shouted Susanna. Suddenly the retreat turned into a flight. The boys, seeing themselves alone exchanging blows with the police and the soldiers, who had debussed and were preparing to advance, began to run off towards San Floreano or towards Borgo Romans.

They made off just as they had a year or two before when they were discovered by the owners stealing peaches or grapes in a field. And as they ran they gave shouts that were almost joyful, because to manage to escape was also a victory over the police. Those who ran through Borgo Romans also scattered, some to the right and some to the left of the level-crossing, along the railway line to Portogruaro or into the courtyards of the houses.

Others again went lower down through the village to where the first fields began with the bare vines along the terraces. A whole little group from Ligugnana went that way, running fast and chattering excitedly. Two or three wanted to keep on through the fields – to the wood at Marzins maybe – and to wait there for evening until things had quietened down; others wanted to stop in some of the houses near by. In fact it was raining harder and they were soaked, their hair plastered on their foreheads and their jackets dripping.

So wet was the big red scarf Nini wore knotted round his neck that it was almost purple and hung heavily on his breast. But he didn't mind and had not lost any of his pride. Nini was one of those who would have liked to stop there and not go on running through the fields in the rain; at the thought of the police he shrugged his shoulders and made a contemptuous noise with his mouth. 'What can they do,' he said, 'they won't be like the Germans any more.' At that moment they were joined by Eligio, by Onorino and by Livo, who, covering their heads with their jackets, came up with their father along the muddy road between the houses in the doors of which the old women stood watching with their hands on their laps, and the girls, in a state of excitement, talked laughing and shouting.

'What are you doing here?' said Eligio to Nini and the others. 'Come on, get away from here.'

'Where are we to go?' said Nini.

'You don't want to stand here in the rain. Come home and wait till it stops.'

'Let's go,' said Nini.

They all set off, pleased at the decision, walking with great strides, chattering, along a lane between two cottages with stone walls dark with smoke and damp. For a short distance they followed a small ditch with bright green banks after which, towards the fields, there came a row of hazel-trees and of reddish osiers, and they soon arrived at the big cottage where the Pereissons lived.

There was great excitement in the courtyard. The women shouted from the lofts or from the byre; other men and boys who had returned from the demonstration were standing in the doorways or under the eaves.

'Go in, go into the house,' said Eligio. In the kitchen there was scarcely room for them, standing there in embarrassment, among the poor chairs, the long worm-eaten table and the sideboard with the photographs stuck into the glass. It was dark. There was no fire in the clean fireplace.

'I can't even ask you to sit down,' said Eligio's mother, blushing a little under her old wrinkled skin and black scarf. 'There are so many of you.'

'We're a team,' said Nini cheerfully. They stood there for a while in the dark kitchen, still excited, waiting for news from the village, which naturally did not change — those who arrived in small groups always said that the square was still full of police and all the demonstrators had scattered here and there. It was best to wait till evening and then go away unseen.

In spite of this the boys were still waiting for something; they continually went to the door, discussed heatedly and laughed. But gradually, since time was passing and there was nothing new, they calmed down. 'Why don't we go into the byre,' said Eligio; 'we can pass the time better there in the warmth.' 'Take off your jackets,' said Eligio's mother, 'then Alba and I will light the fire and dry them for you.'

Embarrassed and amused, the boys took off their light jackets and in their shirt-sleeves went out into the courtyard and ran into the byre. It was a little byre because the Pereissons didn't have much. At the manger there were two cows and in a corner, behind a partition, a calf. The boys sat on the stools or on some clean straw. After a while four of them began to play at *mora* as a joke at first and then, as they got excited, they began to have a match. Eligio got up: 'I'm going to draw some wine,' he said in dialect. He came back right away with a bottle of his red wine and a pack of cards which he borrowed from a neighbour. At the sight good spirits filled the boys' hearts. In the damp, warm semi-darkness of the byre they prepared to enjoy a game of cards, sitting on the stone floor round a stool which served as a table. The expressions of defiance which the opposing couples exchanged were in fact expressions of deep joy, of ill-concealed satisfaction. Everyone was playing in the byre – some at *mora*, some at cards – with great concentration and the old enthusiasm of the winter evenings. Time passed only too quickly. Only Onorino did not play and watched with his English army shirt open on his chest and his short peasant's trousers.

Then the time came to see to the cows and Onorino helped Eligio with the work while the others, continuing to play, poked fun at them. Eligio replied cheerfully in kind and Onorino laughed silently looking about him merrily. When they had finished working with their spades on the fresh dung and with their forks on the mangers, Eligio, instead of resuming his place to play, went and lay down on a heap of hay. He did not feel well, perhaps because of the labours of the day and the way he had been drenched. His eyes were still merry but very, very small and his drawn skin was like an old man's; but he wasn't one to be cast down and he laughed at the touch of fever he felt.

He was the one who sent Onorino to see what was going on outside.

The rain had stopped. Indeed, behind the mountains which were only fifty kilometres or so from San Giovanni and which stood out along the horizon, grey and white, like a row of altars, the sky had cleared. In contrast to this background, which was supremely bright and seemed to be filled to the brink with the peace of the night, the byres and houses were dark, of a deep chestnut colour, smoky and dripping with moisture. The trees in the gardens and fields stood round in hopeless immobility.

Onorino ran lightly, jumping the puddles in the street while around him there spread, along with the smell of toasted polenta and of damp faggots burning on the hearths, the usual noise of supper.

On the street too there were people, very much like any other evening.

Gradually as one got closer to the square the activity ceased, but not entirely. In the square the worst was over. There were people out shopping and a lot of girls taking the milk to the dairy on their bicycles with the pails ringing gaily against their handlebars. Further on, in Borgo Braida, the workers' club was closed and in front of the porch, which led to the courtyard where the demonstrators' bicycles were heaped, stood two or three police with a few inquisitive little boys around them. But the courtyard was not packed with bicycles as it had been before, in fact one wall was by now completely empty. That meant that many had already left.

Onorino ran back to Romans: he had good news and couldn't wait to tell it. The others were still there playing in the byre in their shirt-sleeves, immersed in their games, with their eyes shining from the wine they had drunk from the Pereissons' little glasses.

'It's all over,' said Onorino as he came in with his pretty, honest little boy's face, full of ill-concealed enthusiasm, 'the police aren't saying anything.'

The others stopped playing, perhaps a little disappointed and showing themselves to be worried and distrustful at the boy's optimism. They asked him a lot of questions to which he replied, full of the importance of his role as bearer of tidings and of the sense of joy he felt at his news. Everything was over now; everything was back to normal.

'Come on, let's go,' said Nini, the first as usual. 'We won't have to wait here till tomorrow morning.'

'Besides, what can they do to us?' he added. 'Even if they were to stop us, it's all over.'

Their light, darned jackets, which had been hung in heaps on the backs of the chairs round the Pereissons' hearth, were dry. The Ligugnana boys slipped them on, making quite a din, with Eligio and Onorino's mother standing watching with her hands on her lap and Alba and the other girls standing red-faced in a corner of the big kitchen.

'Goodbye, signora, and thank you,' the boys from Ligugnana shouted from the door. 'Goodbye, Eligio.'

'Goodbye, boys,' said Eligio, burning with fever, laughing with his hands in his pockets. 'Goodbye, goodbye,' the others shouted still, turning round as they crossed the courtyard. 'Goodbye,' said Eligio again. 'Good luck.'

The evening was darker already and in the clear part of the sky some stars shone.

Borgo Braida was still much more deserted than the rest of the village. The long line of grey stone cottages stretched in both directions like ramparts with doors shut and no lights in the windows.

Silent and in suspense the boys from Ligugnana approached the workers' club ready to turn back if things went badly. They walked in single file along the narrow pavement past the worm-eatern doors, beneath the little dark windows of the byres. The door of the workers' club was open and a rectangle of melancholy yellow light sizzled on the mud.

The boys passed quickly and in silence in front of the door of the club, and they saw in the bar, among the frayed straw chairs on the wet floor, two or three policeman drinking some of the club's white wine as an aperitif. The police saw them but showed no interest.

Then, before the others could change their minds, Nini and the others, cheerfully and quickly went into the courtyard where their bicycles were the only ones left, piled on top of one another.

They took them and, once in the street, mounted them in silence and pedalled quietly through Borgo Braida.

At that moment the bells began to ring for evening service and their din was the louder for the silence all around, but now it was the silence of every evening, the evenings of San Giovanni, of Casarsa, of San Floreano, of Gruaro, of all the villages round about. In between the peals of the bells near by one could, in fact, hear, far off, other bells like them but strangely plangent, incomprehensible, almost magical, as if their distant murmur came from the heart of other, past ages.

When the Ligugnana boys passed in front of the church, through the half-open door, along with the trembling, damp and reddish light, there distinctly came from the interior of the church the sound of the hymns the women were shouting:

Living bread of heaven
great sacra-a-a-ment

And the peals overhead were stronger and stronger and seemed to shake the poor stone walls of San Giovanni.

Then the boys, who were rapidly approaching the last houses of the village, scattered among the vineyards and the last stalks of maize along the road to Gruaro, and so as not to accept defeat, began to sing too, with all their might, with voices that were lost in the silence of the cold and greenish fields, 'The Red Flag'.

PART TWO
1949

IX

It was a Sunday afternoon. All the Faedis girls had gone on ahead to Rosa for vespers. Only Cecilia and the smallest girl, Ilde, were still at home getting ready to the accompaniment of rebukes from the older ones. Cecilia was putting a new dress on for the first time and she was all excited.

Some girls who lived in a little hamlet still more lost in the countryside came by to pick them up. They were less conventional and gayer girls than the Faedis – they weren't going to vespers but to dance.

The Faedis' house was built of stone. You entered by a big gate that gave on to the courtyard where for years unused equipment – wheels, hoe-handles, ploughshares – had become covered with dust and rotted away. But on Sunday everything had a new, shining look under the still strong October sun and there was not a piece of straw or a maize stalk to be seen. The men and the boys were out and the light lay peacefully on the trees in the garden, which by now were bare but still full of birds.

Cecilia and her little sister slept in the same tiny room on the ground floor between the kitchen and the living-room. The only window, which looked towards the mountains, was in the damp shadow of a small ditch along which the lane, very muddy at this point, passed.

'Cecilia, Cecilia!' her friends cried from there. She appeared on the little balcony with her hair still undone in one hand and a comb in the other.

'It's early, girls,' she shouted. 'Come in!' They came round the house and into the little room.

'Are you still here?' they asked loudly and indignantly.

'I can't help it. Don't leave me behind!' said Cecilia almost laughing.

'Oh, get it over and done with!' said Ines.

Cecilia was still doing her hair, twisting the braid round her little lamb's head with the combs held firmly in her lips. She soon finished and took from the clothes-chest the new red dress, which was almost dazzling, and the more it dazzled the more it awoke the admiration of her friends.

'We have to baptize it!' they shouted as they helped Cecilia to put it on. Once Cecilia was ready, they all went into the big room, laughing like mad.

When they heard them the women of the house muttered something, but also in a jolly mood. Cecilia took the rubber tube, put it in a barrel and, sucking it, made the red wine spurt out. They drank almost a glass each and they came out of the room laughing even louder.

'Get a move on!' shouted Giuditta, Cecilia's mother. 'They're ringing the bells for the service.'

From Rosa there came the sound of the bells. The house was almost a kilometre from the village and the individual peals spread across the countryside, lonely and pure.

It was almost four o'clock and there was already a lot going on in the one long street in Rosa. Youths were racing past on their bicycles or else they stood in front of the inns. They came from Casarsa, from Valvasone, from San Lorenzo and even from further off. Some were already standing in the square astride their bicycles in front of the council building; but the boys who looked after the bicycles were not ready yet.

'I wonder if he'll come!' said the girls.

'Who'll come?' asked Ilde.

'The one from Ligugnana,' shouted Ines laughing.

Cecilia blushed and pretended not to hear.

The cinema hall, where there was dancing on Sundays, was at the beginning of the village. Just there the street made a slight curve so that from it you could see almost the whole embankment, high and green, on which a little old church with a low campanile, a little to one side, glowed pink in the sun which was already slightly veiled. The young boys were playing on the embankment waiting for the service to begin. But the old women dressed in black were already going in.

Shortly afterwards the boys of the orchestra, 'the Florita', from Valvasone arrived on their bicycles. They were all a little drunk and, holding their instruments tightly in their arms, they were singing or joking with the youths they knew from other villages.

Cecilia and her friends stopped for a little in the square in front of the hall.

'Come in, never mind – come on!' said Ines. Ilde looked at her and her sister Cecilia with a stern expression.

'Yes!' said Cecilia grimly.

The youths began to go into the hall, leaving their bicycles parked in the courtyard. The first, bolder girls also began to go in. At the back of the hall you could hear the instruments tuning up and the saxophonist striking up the song about how he didn't want to sing American.

Cecilia's friends were impatient to go in. 'Come on in with us for a moment at least!' they said to her. Cecilia glanced at her sister, who still had a disapproving look. 'Just for a minute!' she exclaimed. So they passed through the courtyard, happy but aggressive, under the glances of the boys from other villages.

On the stage the orchestra was ready but there were still only a few girls and the boys, in knots round the walls, were ready to assail them the moment the first number began.

Near a column was Nini, with a group of friends, with his usual carefree air, his face red from the sun, the cold and work. He was almost absent-minded and kept his hands buried in the pockets of his new, well-ironed grey trousers, his Sunday best.

Cecilia's companions looked at her and put on a special expression. They nudged her with their elbows and said: 'There he is!'

The orchestra had struck up gaily with a *paso doble* which sounded even louder in the almost empty hall, but behind the music you could hear the bells ringing to announce the beginning of the service.

'Goodbye, goodbye, girls,' said Cecilia, pushing her sister out of the hall. 'Did you see the one from Ligugnana?' said Ilde.

Cecilia had a terrified look. She repented of having entered the hall; she had never done it before. And that old woman from next door might have seen her. Outside, the bell sounded in a melancholy way; the embankment was deserted. And the light of the sun, already low, slanted down from a cloudless sky, skimming across the almost too green countryside, across the village cottages, patched with damp and crumbling after the fierce heat of the summer, across the deserted orchards, the grey courtyards in the midst of which, among the disorder of the hen-coops and pig-sties, a few old mulberry-trees blazed forth. Now you could feel that evening was near.

In a few months much had changed. First of all Nini had found work — to be precise, through the help of his friend Castellarin, who worked at the Mangiarotti factory. Nini had been working in the explosives store and had changed quite a lot. He had always been a progressive youth. Now he looked like someone from the city — well dressed, always jolly and with a superior air.

He, too, like Eligio and Milio, should have gone off to do his military service, but of the three only Eligio would perhaps have had to join up if his health hadn't played up. It wasn't a question of invaliding him out, but lately he had got thinner and thinner and was all skin and bone. The fault of the storm. There had been a storm that summer and it had ruined the harvest, at the time when Eligio and Nini were in Yugoslavia. So when they came home Eligio had found things twice as bad as before, for the smallholders had suffered most from the storm. The two small fields of maize and vines on which all the Pereissons lived had been half destroyed by the hail and the family hardly knew how to survive. Debts and poverty . . . so Eligio had gone to work in a quarry over towards Cordovado, which had sucked his blood and spirit.

Eligio was the eldest of the brothers and for that reason should have done his military service. Nini was excused, because he was an only son; the others were dead, one from an illness as a little boy, and two in the war, in Albania. And Milio was the youngest in his family and his older brothers had done their service.

The only people for whom things had not changed but remained the same were the Faedis. Home and church, home and church – of course nothing changed. If you have no demands you have no disappointments either! In fact all the Faedis, young and old, were enjoying a happy and exciting time because the day was drawing near when Regina was to marry Ernesto Castellarin. The wedding was to take place in the spring. And now it was winter. In the fields there was little to do – at the most there were the maize stalks to cut down or some little job for which there was no hurry in the courtyard or in the garden.

Now it was getting dark early. When the Angelus bell rang from Rosa the countryside was deserted and the supper fires gleamed on the old steps of the doorways.

At the separate, heavy, sonorous peals which announced the evening service, the whole Faedis house echoed although it was far from the village. But between the plain, vast and cool under the first stars, and the circle of the mountains, the air was so pure that even the peals of the most distant bells were borne along through it: the twin bells of Gruaro, the shrill and piercing ones of San Floreano, those of Casarsa, very far off.

In the Faedis' house then the usual voices were raised. 'Get a move on, the children are waiting!' the old women shouted from the kitchen.

'Yes, yes, keep quiet!' the girls answered from Cecilia's bedroom.

'So you have the cheek to answer back, eh?' shouted one of the old women as if she were on edge.

'I don't care!' shouted Ilde.

As on every evening the girls had to go to the kindergarten in Rosa.

Cecilia, Ilde and all the others were Daughters of Mary and so had a lot to do with the nuns at the kindergarten. These were very special relationships in which the friendship – which, as always between peasant women, was very simple and boisterous – stopped at a certain point, because beyond it there extended in all its vastness the realm of the Lord.

In character the nuns were just like the girls, like Regina, for example, and the older ones were very little different from the housewives, even physically. They were great chatterboxes, secretly loving company and a jolly half-hour and even they had their weaknesses.

One of their main concerns was to maintain an exemplary modesty in praying, in clasping their hands, in swallowing the consecrated bread and in all such matters — in short, to keep themselves constantly in the state of mind which we see in the most modern saints, such as Don Bosco and Santa Rica da Cascia. On the other hand, since they were forced every day to take part in the humble and common tasks of the kindergarten, they had not completely overcome their resemblance to women of their mental level, which was not very high, given that they too came from peasant families from the Veneto or even from Friuli.

Notwithstanding the fact that they were on an equal footing, there was something that made them seem distant and happy compared to the girls. The latter had sweet, respectful and refined images of the nuns. Each one had her favourite and, since they were very close, each one had the one she liked least. Regina loved Sister Maria; Cecilia, Sister Celeste. Sometimes they criticized them openly and cheerfully when they were spinning in the byre, but always, underlying their criticism, was the firmly rooted impression of something divine emanating from the nuns as if they were persons whose life had been fixed once and for all, a little like the little figures of the saints, of the Sacred Heart, the Madonna, the Infant Jesus.

The girls took from all this a sense of religious inferiority and at this point their friendship with the nuns found its natural boundary and each one withdrew into that field that had been assigned for her — as if they were on different sides of a river: on this side, the girls, subject to mad fits of merriment, to the ill-concealed hope of marrying a good-looking boy, to quarrels with their cousins; on the other, in a white light, the nuns — also by no means without human weaknesses — but invested with a destiny which was mysterious and a little romantic.

Cecilia and the other Faedis girls didn't only visit the nuns for reasons to do with church. They went to help them during the summer as well when children came to be given an open-air cure, or else they went to them to learn to embroider, to patch clothes or learn other women's work or, finally, in turn, to accompany the little ones of the family to the kindergarten.

As they did every evening the Faedis girls went towards the village in the dark, arm in arm and walking quickly.

The kindergarten was not far from the church just at the point where the street widened in front of the cinema and branched by the porch of the town hall. It was a little pink building with big patches of damp, behind it a courtyard shaded by large chestnut-trees.

As they walked along, the girls were silent and well behaved. Only when they were in sight of the first houses of the village did Regina, who was soon to be married and so had gained in dignity and wisdom, shout gaily as she saw a group of youths leaning on their bicycles near the square: 'Be quiet, children, these stupid boys are there!'

Cecilia made herself very small, grasping with greater dignity the little black veil she held folded in her hand; but the others, heedless of her indifference, began to walk more uprightly, holding each other tighter by the arm, even if they could not refrain from an occasional impetuous gesture, which revealed their curiosity, their excitement, and their determination to pay no attention to anything except the nuns who awaited them.

They walked directly towards the kindergarten because on the grass of the embankment, around the low wall, there were, collected along with the other little Catholic boys, their cousins and brothers who had to go to confession. But at the corner of the street in front of the worm-eaten door of the cinema, where the youths stood in the mud with their bicycles, there was no doubt that something was bound to happen. 'There are the Faedis girls!' a youngster from Braida shouted ironically.

The girls went on their way proudly, trying only to avoid the ruts which gleamed with water.

'You ugly things!' the boy repeated jokingly. Ilde could not contain herself and to the alarm but also with the tacit approval of the others – she could do it after all because she wasn't fourteen yet – shouted: 'You'll be ugly too!'

'Listen to her, she's still at the breast!' said another boy from Braida. Ilde, wounded to the quick, with a knot in her throat, went on walking arm in arm with the others, trying to match her steps to the dignity of the big girls.

The boys laughed. At that moment the little door of the nearby tobacconist's, with its dusty windows and lines of cigarette packets, opened, and Ernesto, Regina's fiancé, and 'the boy from Ligugnana' came out together. Both were lighting their cigarettes and stopped there among the others. Ernesto only smiled, with a slight greeting for Regina, who blushed with pleasure and greeted him softly in return. Nini leant against the door-post with his blouse unbuttoned and his hands in his trouser pockets.

He watched in silence, ironically, smoking his cigarette. When two or three striplings took their bicycles and began to ride round the line of girls, brushing against them and making them lose some of their proud bearing, he took a step into the street, detaching himself a little from his companion, and when the Faedis passed in front of him said in a voice that was almost inaudible and with a smile that wrinkled his brow: 'Ciao, don't you recognize me?'

But the girls took to their heels towards the kindergarten and this revived Ilde's courage and she began to shout at the little boys who were following them — as they deserved — 'Idiots, stupid boys, go to bed!'

The boys, after following them up as far as the little wall round the kindergarten, where they could hear the voices of the children saying their prayers together, turned back towards the door of the cinema with their bicycles, which they cheerfully abandoned in the mud, and their coloured scarves tied tightly round their necks, fluttered in the patch of light from the electric lamp in the tobacconist's.

Ernesto was a good-looking boy, blond, already balding a little, with the skin of his forehead slightly red where the hair was thin. He was the only one wearing an overcoat, chestnutty in colour, which he took great care of. Now he was there laughing as he watched the girls run away.

'They didn't so much as look at you,' he said to Nini, laughing.

'What does that matter to me!' said Nini, shrugging cheerfully without the least shadow of annoyance. He went towards his bicycle and with a push and a run leapt on to it. Two or three other mates from work came out of the tobacconist's and all together they began to cycle down towards San Floreano in the direction from which the girls had come. They rode along chatting and whistling very quietly as they did every evening on their way back from the powder factory, going in single file along the side of the road, which was the only dry part, by the edge of the canal.

When they reached the Faedis' cottage standing by itself among the bare thickets and the fields, Ernesto said goodbye to the company, took the lane that led to the house and went in to wait till Regina came back with her cousins from the village.

The others quickly arrived at San Floreano and, as they did almost every evening, went into the biggest inn of the hamlet. They sat at a table, ordered a litre and began to play at *mora*.

They hadn't been there long when one of the dark-haired boys looked up from the table, and wiping his sweat away and gaping in astonishment, said: 'Look at that, eh!'

Nini and the others then turned round lazily and saw that he was talking about a beautiful girl sitting there. She was really beautiful – of a rare beauty.

'Who is it?' said Nini. 'Pia?'

The beauty sat there behind the old discoloured and encrusted bar between a dusty glass jar full of sweets and the brass scales. She sat with her shoulders against the shelves, which were full of little bottles of liqueurs and orangeades, and read, looking very tidy and elegant with her long smooth hair which reached her shoulders over the little dark red dress.

She was a big girl already, this Pia; she was twenty-two or twenty-three although she looked younger, being thin and pale with a pair of eyes so black that they even darkened the surrounding skin of her face, which was pale and sweet as the moon.

Nini knew her because he had seen her when she was small – that is when she was sixteen or seventeen – when he was just beginning to go to inns with the grown-ups and was left in a corner to drink his orangeade. Then Pia had left for the city, which was the very opposite of what everyone else was doing, for people were evacuating the cities to come to the country. But she had an aunt in Padua or Mestre or Verona and hoped to set herself up there – or so they said. What she had done then no one knew. There was gossip going about but no one could say anything. Now Pia sang on Sundays with the little orchestra in a dance-hall in Pordenone, but this was only recently and Nini hadn't been there yet. This evening was the first time he had ever seen her again.

He left his companions round the table, which was dirty with wine, and went up to the bar.

'You are Pia!' he said.

The girl raised her eyes from her illustrated magazine *Grand Hotel* as if she were waking from sleep, looked at him sweetly and almost as if she were in tears, and said politely: 'Yes.'

'I knew you before you went away!' said Nini boldly.

Pia smiled.

'What are you up to now? I hear you sing – '

Pia passed a hand over her extremely long smooth hair, slightly embarrassed, but not like those girls who in moments of embarrassment adjust their hair with a movement of the head like hens pecking. She passed her hand down from her forehead along that river of black hair as if she had a slight headache and that was all. And she smiled again: 'Yes, I sing at Pordenone,' she said very modestly.

Nini was like a full bottle which, wanting to pour out all its wine at once, instead pours only a tiny drop because the neck is narrow. Dance-halls, orchestras, singers – imagine that! They were all things that were like a light inside him – the light which had always made him different from the others so that when he came into a dance he was one of those who gave it life just by his presence. He had always been like that, a town boy not a peasant boy. Like Pia. And so he began to talk about all these things with his elbows on the bar and the black lock on his forehead: ballrooms, orchestras, singers –

'Do you know Nello, the violinist of the "Fiorita" of Valvasone?'

'Y-es, I have sung with him too.'

'He's good! We've known each other for a long time! Eh, I don't miss a single dance. At Gruaro, at Casarsa, at Casale, at San Floreano – everywhere. Specially at this time of year – at carnival. What's the new dance-hall at Pordenone like? I haven't been there yet!'

'It's ever so nice. A really posh place.'

'I'm going on Sunday. With my mates if they can. Maybe we'll hire a car. So we'll come and clap you when you sing!'

Pia looked at him with wide-open eyes, which were starry and a little moist against that dry skin of hers that was like the skin of a page-boy or an angel.

'I'm not someone posh who can afford to drive about in a car. But just once won't be the end of the world. You know what it's like — that's how we poor workingmen get along!'

'Do you work?'

'Yes at Mangiarotti's — at the powder factory,' said Nini proudly.

'That's dangerous,' Pia remarked, frowning a little like a good, sensible girl, and once again giving a slight shake to her Hawaiian hair.

'I don't care!' exclaimed Nini. 'You only die once! Eh,' he added. 'If I want to eat I have to work!'

'That's how it is!' said Pia.

'This bloody government,' said Nini. 'Oilè, oilè, oilè and with de Gasperi you don't eat,' he sang lightly because usually women don't want to hear any mention of politics. But Pia said simply and gracefully: 'Eh, socialism will be on the up and up!'

'Will you come back from Pordenone in the car with us?' Nini said then dashingly, for he had a great desire to hug her.

And she said simply, at once accessible and reserved: 'I'll come.'

'You'll see what a good time we'll have!' said Nini in a new burst of high spirits. He wasn't thinking at that moment of possibly falling in love with this girl; he spoke to her just as a friend, out of liking, because they had the same tastes. He thought perhaps of having a bit of fun with her — certainly not to take her seriously. He just liked her, that was all.

'Why,' he said with a beautiful smile, 'don't you wear a flower on your head? It would suit you with such long hair.'

He took a piece of parsley which was there on the bar along with some other greens in a piece of newspaper and placed it on her head, a little above the ear, on her river of smooth silky hair.

'Look how it suits you!' he cried.

Pia looked at him with *Grand Hotel* in her hands and her big black eyes, which were wide-open and gentle and seemed to be saying: Lassie, go home!

X

In the middle of the Faedis' byre – as in all byres – there was a
stone corridor with runnels for the dung on either side. To right
and left, separated by partitions of filthy, worm-eaten beams,
were the beasts, lying down or standing among the maize-stalks,
which were dripping with dung, and warming the air like stoves.

In the centre of the corridor, under the small lamp, which
dangled from the very high ceiling, the women were gathered –
as every evening – sitting in a circle on little stools with baskets
of work between their knees.

Sometimes the men sat up with them too but almost always
they went off to sleep an hour or two earlier. The last to leave
were the boys – those that were neither so small that they fell
asleep on their mothers' knees nor so big that they showed a
manly lack of interest in the women's chat.

So a kind of alliance sprang up directed against the older men,
the heads of the household, and a jolly and somewhat daring
atmosphere was created which even the old women went along
with.

The talk had something excited about it, something reckless
and slightly guilty. Alone but gathered together in the midst of
the countryside which, although compline had just rung, seemed
to be sunk in a deep sleep, they felt an inner shudder of pleasing
fear, of freedom.

They laughed for no reason, especially the young ones, but
were immediately followed good-humouredly by the older

women. The moment the men left — and they all wanted this moment to come quickly, though no one said so and pretended to be very jolly if one of the young boys remained — it was usually the youngest girls who started up the topics of the previous evening about which they had already laughed so much.

Nor was it unusual for one of them to have the courage to suggest going to get some wine and, if the truth be told, they all spent the evening waiting for someone or other to have the courage to put forward this pleasing suggestion. The ones to get up from their seat right away and run into the cellar to fill the little blue jug with wine were almost always Nesto and Osvaldo, the little cousins of the same age, with their trousers half-undone and on their feet only the thick white wool socks made by their sisters. After they had drunk a half-glass of wine, which dyed their lips like paint, the merriment became even more general. Sometimes then they dared to talk about love.

Cecilia and Nini never talked to each other. Perhaps Nini had not even noticed Cecilia's existence. But although this was how things were, her cousins and friends kept on talking about them as if they were sweethearts, or almost so. Cecilia, if by chance she had had such a thought, had for sure never confided it to any living soul and certainly not even to herself. The thought of Nini gave her a kind of feeling of fear — that was all. And this was something she had not even dared to think about to herself far less talk about it. Yet her cousins, especially in the evening, in the byre, never stopped their hints, their pin-pricks. Cecilia became deep red and spoke no more. She left it to Ilde to take up her defence.

But one evening Regina, laughing and full of mischief and shyness, told her boy Ernesto about 'it' while they were passing one of their long and chaste evenings by the fireside, where the Faedis left them alone although obviously keeping an eye on them.

Ernesto, laughing too, passed it on to Nini at work. And Nini was flattered and had him explain exactly who Cecilia was.

'She's a pretty young thing,' he thought. 'Wait and I'll do something about it.'

He began to pay some attention to how the Faedis girls took turns to take the milk to the dairy and, on Cecilia's evening, he positioned himself on the road a little out of the village, waiting for her to go back home across the frozen fields, which were almost black in spite of the last flaming beams of the sunset way across the plain.

Cecilia appeared down the road among the last low walls and last houses of the village, coming along the white road with the milk-cans banging on her handlebars – like a little angel with those two tresses framing her lamb's face.

Nini waited astride his bicycle for her to pass in front of him and then began to pedal along at her side on the dry mud.

Cecilia looked in front of her with staring eyes as if she had seen nothing.

'Good evening, signorina!' said Nini, who was twice her size, pedalling along very slowly with his legs splayed a little.

Since she said nothing he went on: 'We know each other! I am Nini Infant, Ernesto's mate.'

It was terrible for Cecilia. She said nothing, as if she were suffocated, but she did not blink, with her little face red from the cold under the great tresses. She looked straight ahead – that was all. She would have liked to run away – to be dead.

Nini thought she was saying nothing in the usual way girls say nothing, from a sense of duty, out of coquetry, and went on: 'You are the prettiest of all the Faedis girls! I've been looking at you for ages!'

He pedalled a little quicker to look in her face. No expression of either displeasure or pleasure or fear was to be seen there. She seemed blind or deaf. It was as if he did not exist.

'Do you mind if I come with you a bit on your way home?' asked Nini, beginning to lose heart a little.

The road was entirely deserted. A few nude stalks of millet, a few branches of elder, a tangle of thin osiers, red as blood, stuck up here and there on the bank of the canal. There was no sight or sound of anyone. Then, through the air, which was sonorous with cold, there began to ring the compline bells.

'Can we see each other some other time?' asked Nini. But Cecilia, in a state of terror, did not answer. She had become white and trembled all over, although it did not show.

'Have you lost your tongue?' Nini asked then, a little impatiently, using the familiar form of address, and speaking to her suddenly as one speaks to a little girl.

Now between the rows of bare vines the black silhouette of the Faedis' house stood out.

'Then I'm going back – you don't want me!' said Nini still as if he was talking to a little girl. Cecilia pedalled on saying nothing and with her face immobile, looking desperately towards her home. Then he stopped and prepared to turn round and go back.

'Goodbye!' he said a little ironically as he watched her move away. He had not managed to drag out of her a word or a smile, not even a glance. He shrugged and went back whistling towards the village with its lights shining against the fields.

On the day of the official engagement of Regina and Ernesto there was a big stir at the Faedis' house.

The companions of both the boy and the girl came and since it was the coldest time of the winter the old people were at home, having nothing to do in the fields.

Among Ernesto's friends there was Nini as well as friends of longer standing, from childhood. There was hardly room in the big kitchen. Many of them were round the hearth; others stood along the walls round the dresser with the photographs stuck into the glass.

There was Eligio too, wilder than ever, with that hair of his above his burning eyes; he had brought his accordion. He began to play gaily: 'When the cock crows . . . ' and then boogie-woogie. The old folks of the Faedis household had drunk a glass or two extra for the occasion so when the young people indicated that they wanted to hop about, at first they opposed it weakly like the true Catholics they were, then gave their consent – but just for a little while.

Cecilia was huddled in a corner on a stone of the hearth. And she looked and looked with her big lamb's eyes as if she wanted to make herself small, to disappear.

Nini danced a bit with everyone, even with the older women, who tried to put him off, bursting with laughter and clapping their hands over their mouths. But he did not go and pick Cecilia – as if he had not seen her. He had put on his best trousers, the grey ones, well ironed, and while he danced he seemed even stronger and more elegant. In any case Cecilia had so little opinion of herself that she was not even disappointed, because to be so she would have had to hope that Nini would ask her and instead she did not even dare to think of it.

She enjoyed herself all the same, just as she was, seeing Nini dancing with her aunt Anuta, toothless and a bit drunk, or with Ilde who didn't reach up to his trouser-belt.

At last Nini made up his mind, a little unsure of himself, perhaps discouraged by the memory of that evening when he had tried to talk to her. Red as fire, laughing only because the others were laughing, but with a smile that was on the edge of tears, Cecilia accepted. She didn't know how to dance very well — up to now she had danced only with her sisters and cousins and she was taking great care not to make any mistakes.

She was close against him; she felt his chest, his thighs as if they were not real and their weight and power there by accident and so much part of him that their presence was almost miraculous; it made her feel not so much shy as frightened.

They danced until late. The youths, half-drunk and singing, went off because the moon was already high over the countryside, which was almost blue.

It was the evening of Epiphany and it was an evening of great excitement in the Faedis' byre among the women who were there spinning.

There was a special air of merriment, partly because they had visitors — a young wife and the Owl, that chatterbox with her little girl's voice whom no one could silence, who had come from nearby cottages. For two hours there was nothing but talk, laughter, noise, so much so that although the little boys might have been dying of sleep they did not intend to lose a word of this evening of merriment.

Even when the talk became difficult, serious, with allusions and judgements which were of direct interest only to the grown-ups they drank in the meaning and made it theirs as a matter of course, without taking sides, with that spirit of good-natured humbleness they had inherited from their parents. If it was a question of defending the Church against modern life and Communism, of praising life in the old days in contrast to the bad manners and easy-going ways of the youth of today, all the Faedis were in agreement even if they were not absolute bigots.

But the Owl was more argumentative and that evening had the courage to oppose the whole lot of the Faedis. But the Faedis, especially the women, laughed at her for they knew her character very well and instead of replying said to her, red with laughter: 'Be quiet, madwoman, be quiet!'

But the Owl had taken off and with her flow of talk overwhelmed them all. She had a little girl's voice so shrill that you could hear it two kilometres away when she quarrelled with her husband.

Now, while remaining firm in her attachment to the Church and with her piety as a good Christian beyond discussion, she had begun to protest about the government and very nearly to defend Communists. The women, shocked and amused, almost shouting by now and jokingly pretending to take off a clog, went on repeating: 'Be quiet, madwoman, be quiet.'

And for a while the men with laughter frozen in their eyes put up with her, then they began to contradict her jokingly and, finally, Cecilia's uncle, Erminio, who was a character too, with his hoarse loud voice, began to take on the job of putting her in her place.

But she didn't give in, lifted up her head like a cock and, little and round as she was, represented a real threat to the prestige of big Erminio, who could not defend himself against her shrill cries. The Owl argued without minding in the least that she contradicted herself or said stupid things as long as she won the argument.

Then Erminio, loading his pipe with as much noise as a locomotive, thought it time to get to grips with her by giving her facts and examples: 'The Communists,' he said, pulling on his pipe with clouds of smoke that hissed like a damp log, 'are all criminals, people who do not want to work! Just look at Rosa here or San Giovanni, you mad thing, look who they are. Jacu, the son of Sante Miòr, Rico Quarnùs and all those windbags – Nin Giacomùs, Sigi Pereisson, Pieri Susanna. A fine lot! And then look at the outsiders, the ones that work at Mangiarotti's. Take a look at them! Just tell me, if you had a daughter to marry off would you give her to one of them. Eh? Someone like Nini

Infant,' he added, 'would you let him have her?'

'All people without religion!' old Anuta stressed.

Cecilia listened with her eyes downcast, as motionless as a picture, while all the Faedis nodded, even Francesco, father of Cecilia and Ilde, who was usually more open-minded and jovially calm.

But the Owl had lost her desire to talk about politics and vented her last polemical feelings, showing that she did not accept these arguments and at the same time demonstrating that no one called her tune, by beginning to sing at the top of her voice one of the two or three songs she liked best:

> You can't always be merry
> Nor always s-a-a-a-d.

Hearing her sing in that half-strangled way, all red with the effort, they all began to laugh, beginning with the little boys. The women laughed without restraint and so did the girls. Ilde gave deafening shrieks, worse than the boys, and even Cecilia, although calm, with eyes that were staring and a little frightened, laughed and laughed.

Then the Owl and the other neighbours went off and the men too went up to bed, making the whole house shake.

The Faedis women, however, stayed on to make up for the time lost chattering and began to work fast in a group under the lamp. Every so often they remembered things said and done during the evening and they laughed again, then gradually a great silence fell on the byre.

Cecilia did not raise her eyes again from the linen she was mending, not even at the last scattered bursts of merriment. She sat there bent, with her hair pulled over her brow and the long tresses hanging heavily down her back. She had a child's face, perhaps from sleep or the heat, and her lamb's eyes shone more tenderly. Then the oldest of the Faedis women went to the door of the byre for a moment to get a breath of air. She had half-opened it and you could see a piece of night sky shining like silk. The old woman had stayed there a while pulling her big black scarf over her forehead and, looking up in the profound silence, exclaimed in dialect: 'Ring round the moon keeps rain away.'

At that very moment Cecilia let her work fall to the ground on to the stones and ran out of the byre. The door remained wide open and you could see the whole sky, empty, white, and in the midst the moon caught in its halo and some clouds as light as dust. The women looked at one another in amazement and the old woman from the doorway cried across the courtyard: 'Cecilia! Cecilia!' Regina and Cecilia's mother quickly laid their work down in their baskets and went after her to see what had happened. But they found her already in her little room, stretched out with her face in the mattress, sobbing.

XI

Pia often went to Gruaro either to do some shopping or to go to
the hairdresser's to have a perm. She went by bicycle. Nini often
waited for her after work, cycling quickly down from Rosa by the
main road, and went back to San Floreano with her.

Their love, which to begin with – to tell the truth – was not
very serious, had become stronger and stronger. But Nini did not
think about it and was still convinced that he was going with Pia
only to have a bit of fun. He had had lots of girls and this one,
although he liked her better, was like all the others as far as that
went. But Pia, when it came to having fun, did not go beyond a
certain point and seemed to have no intention at all of giving in.

She was decent, a good girl – so what did it all mean: that
sultry, fatal look, those big eyes even if they were deeply sunk
beneath her white brow, which looked up, imploring or naïve,
like an actress's eyes, and that long smooth hair that hung down
her back?

Nini was quite at a loss and was amazed each time. He was
quite unable to take in that Pia really was a good girl, perhaps
still a virgin, and that her hopes were set on an engagement and
marriage like all the other girls. And it wasn't even for what she
could get out of it, given that Nini, with all his town boy's airs,
was only a poor workman at Mangiarotti's.

Pia accepted their relationship with a slightly dreamy air as if
it was something happening not to her but to one of the girls in
her romantic stories and was constantly silent and well-behaved.

When he tried anything on she defended herself, more sad and pained than offended, but it was clear that she had a long experience of defending herself. She must have known a good few men.

One evening when, as on other occasions, they were cycling back from Gruaro, Nini was beyond himself with desire to make love to her. And he pedalled silently, not speaking.

After Rosa the road to San Floreano was quite deserted, full of bends, a little country road which, in those days, the dry cold made hard and white as it ran between the bare thickets, the rough, red tangles of the osiers and the acacias, which grew in clumps along the ditches.

At one of the bends there was a little bridge with a washing-place under the dry boughs; there they usually stopped to kiss in the dark of the evening.

Nini stopped and, as on other occasions, almost lifted Pia from her bicycle but instead of leaning her against the low wall of the bridge he pushed her down the path by the water towards the washing-place. There was no one there, only a few little autumnal birds flitting about in the branches.

Pia did not resist; she understood that this evening was the evening that had to come sooner or later. Nini laid her down on some grass, partly dry and partly damp, on the side of the ditch among some bushes, some red clumps of osier, and covered her with his big, heavy body.

When he had finished and in his embarrassment did not know where to put his rough hands, used to operating heavy tools or to caressing women very different from Pia, Nini thought with alarm what she might do or say. But Pia, instead, said nothing and did nothing. She only seemed to be saddened and surprised, with a profound look of a victim deep in her eyes.

All around was silence. They could hear only the tiny lost birds, which stay in the fields during winter, flitting about or chirping. They jumped from bough to bough, from a dry elder to a dry mulberry at the far end of the strips between the vines, which were as long as corridors and ended up at the ditch with its frozen water dark against the grass that was the colour of the pale sun. Then suddenly there appeared from among the low trees, with a heavy beat of its wings, a big bird, grey and the size of a dove, which disappeared again among the low trees. It flew away like a dream. 'A buzzard!' said Nini looking after it. 'And damn it I don't have a sling!'

She smiled, leaning slightly on his shoulder and looking at him with sweet melancholy.

From then on she was like that, always the victim of him and of her own weakness and her expression was always reserved and hurt.

She sat for long hours behind the bar at the inn, working or reading her magazines, waiting for Nini, dressed and combed as if for a reception.

One night at the beginning of December the countryside and the village lay in absolute calm, the calm of a night of frost, when the air is blue and transparent and by the light of the moon you can see the blue mountains ridge by ridge.

The explosion was unexpected, as in the days of the bombing of Casarsa. All the windows shook and a few shattered while the booming noise continued. In their poor bedrooms, which shone like mirrors, from beds and mattresses, all the Faedis woke up and jumped to their feet at once. First of all the boys, leaping from their mattresses, which were stuffed with maize-husks, began running about the house.

Everyone ran up to the little windows in the attic and saw at once along the wasteland by the Tagliamento a long streak of flame which – so clear was the night – made even the walls of the byre and the vineyard below them faintly red.

A storehouse must have exploded at Mangiarotti's. That everyone knew at once.

Regina, thinking of Ernesto, who was on shift that night, began to weep and cry out; the other women at once surrounded her to comfort her and try to raise her hope. Meanwhile the youngsters had dressed hastily and were getting ready to cycle towards the scene of the accident.

In a few minutes they were ready and set off followed by the shouts, the advice and warnings of the men and the women. The latter gathered in the byre and began to say the rosary. Meanwhile the men stood in the courtyard in a group and looked towards the red glow of the fire.

All the women were huddled together on stools or kneeling on the pavement round Anuta, who held up the rosary.

Only Regina and Cecilia stood a little apart, almost praying on their own; they seemed bereft of life by anxiety and pain.

It was already beginning to dawn and the sun had already risen when the boys returned. Ernesto was dead with two or three other workmates; the rest — Nini among them — had escaped.

While Regina shrieked in the arms of the women, Cecilia, in despair and on her own, had in those poor innocent eyes of hers, which were full of tears, something like a brief, fleeting gleam of joy.

From that moment on she began to think and to understand something and it frightened her so much that she thought she was lost for ever.

The following Saturday, as every Saturday, she went to confession. It was as if it were the first time and she made a long and anxious examination of her conscience before presenting herself to the confessor, allowing all the little ones, the girls and the old women who filled the benches to go first. At last she made up her mind, approached the grating and trembling recited the Act of Contrition.

She told the priest everything. She said that that night she had been worried only for Nini, that she had thought only of him, and when she had learned that only Ernesto was dead she had had the courage to thank the Lord.

The priest could not but tell her that she had sinned and gravely; as for what she felt for Nini, she must be very careful that it was not a case of an impure and prohibited feeling.

Crushed by these words, Cecilia was dumb and was on the point of tears. But the priest went on speaking and said that if, by God's grace, any feeling can become pure and admissible, then it was enough to have courage and patience. He also wanted to learn from her about this Nini, whom he did not know. With anguish Cecilia stammered out the little she knew, feeling within her another weight, another fear; the time had now come, after keeping it inside herself for so long, to free herself of it. With eyes lowered, in one breath, as if the fault were hers, she said that Nini was a Communist. But to her astonishment the priest did not appear to find this such a grave matter, in fact he almost

113

smiled a little at Cecilia's fear. He remarked that Nini was young, that he had plenty of time before him to change his ideas, and that the one important thing was that he should be a good boy.

Cecilia ran to her bench in front of the statue of the Madonna to say with deep feeling over and over again the penitential prayers, almost as if she were afraid not to show herself to be sufficiently penitent, because, as she prayed, she felt not pain but, in the bottom of her heart, a strange, sweet, irrepressible joy.

A few primroses were already on the banks of the canals facing the sun and the valerian made the meadows show timidly green against the mountains, which were still white. And so, because winter seemed suddenly to have ended, the last day of carnival was full of trepidation and impatient joy.

That day, in fact, the children of the kindergarten had to perform a play, as every year, before the mayor and the parish priest. So Cecilia and the others got up just as day was breaking, for one thing because they couldn't stay in bed and for another because they wanted to see the carnival procession go past.

In fact, a little later Nisiuti caught sight of it from an attic window. They all ran to see, leaning out of the little peeling window-frames.

From up there they could see a good bit of the plain, to the right Rosa, to the left, much further off, San Floreano, and here and there the belfries of the other villages.

Along the narrow white road that linked Rosa and San Floreano there passed the long masked procession that each year went from Cordovado to Gruaro. There were painted carts on the first of which the 'Fiorita' of Valvasone was giving all it had with saxophone and violin, and behind were groups of masks on foot, carrying on like mad, singing, with huge heads which bobbed up and down as high as the tufts of the osiers on the edge of the ditches.

When the procession, which was very long, had finally passed, the girls, in great excitement, and with their eyes still full of a strange ardour, quickly changed and went swiftly down to the village to the kindergarten, where they had to spend all day preparing for the performance, which took place in the evening after vespers.

The great moment soon arrived – almost too soon. All the children were ready by now with crowns on their heads or wings on their backs, crowded together behind the scenes. But it was unthinkable to leave them to themselves on the stage, especially when they had to dance. Experience showed that even if things went well at the rehearsals, when it came to the performance they would be seized by panic. What a blow to the nuns' self-esteem! So for many years the archangels had been introduced. Having got the children ready and leaving two or three more ambitious ones – perhaps braver than they were – to keep them in place, Cecilia, Ilde and the others, in great elation finished up by running to change in the big workroom on the ground floor.

Laughing, they began to help each other to slip on the long shifts, the same ones as the Daughters of Mary wore at funerals, which had been washed, ruched and decorated with silk sashes. Then they fixed to their shoulders the huge wings with their feathers coloured in layers, white, indigo and purple. And finally they set on their brows, in their hair, a big cardboard star, patiently covered with silver chocolate paper.

'Ah,' said Ilde during this delicate operation, 'to have a perm!'

No one, not even the best behaved, protested at that sigh. They were thinking how good the star would have looked on their brows with their hair done like an angel's or Joan of Arc's. Besides, to see themselves just as they were they had no better mirrors than the windows, which they had opened so that they would reflect the sun well.

They looked at one another trembling because of the touch of cold which had come into the big room along with the bright light from the little sunny square lying between the empty houses and the gardens, and laughed to hide their pleasure at seeing themselves dressed like that in the glass, even if it were so diaphanously that they could scarcely make out in their own images the strawberry colour of their cheeks, which they considered vulgar, the spot of light in their merry eyes, their breasts swollen and hard and scarcely hidden by the thick material.

115

Perhaps because the little glass of vermouth at the reception, with all the mothers and the better-off peasants gathered round the parish priest, had gone to their heads, the Faedis girls had been in a strange holiday humour and all excited.

They took advantage of the fact that they were the least important persons there to permit themselves to behave so freely and gaily that it might have been a little offensive to the others but for their expansive youth. 'Bless the young people!' the parish priest seemed to be saying as he took an almond biscuit from the plate or sipped at the liqueur.

The girls were all bunched together a little to one side, red in the face and silent out of shyness, but ready on the other hand to burst into one of their mysterious peals of laughter, caused by an unimportant gesture by one of their number – the very fact that Ilde opened her mouth and swallowed the vermouth made them laugh.

Yet everything was now over, all so quickly. All that was left of the holiday was the return home across the countryside, where no one was to be seen, along the country roads and the banks of the canals which were tidy and clean. The beadle, for his part, did not bother and without paying the slightest attention to the reception at the nursery school began to ring the bells for the service; and, like little black mice, the old women could be seen on their way to church across the hard earth and the gravel of the square, which had been scoured by the north wind.

When they got back from Mass the Faedis girls had no sooner reached the house than they were overcome by a great feeling of melancholy.

The sun was still a bit high to resign oneself to the end of the day's festivities. Its rays lit up the empty fields, an immense void, from the walls of the old house, from the pump, from the big walnut-tree, to the mountains of the Carnic Alps, as pale as cloths and with a languid light gilding their violet.

How boring, how disappointing! Almost as if to fight against it the girls were seized again by a strange outburst of jollity. They went about the house laughing, here and there doing some work-a-day task, still wearing their new dresses. But the end of it was that the old women promptly chased them up to their bedrooms to change. They ran upstairs stamping with their bare feet on the wooden steps, which smelt sweetly clean.

'Mad things! mad things!' the women shouted from down below.

Suddenly Ilde disappeared. And the others heard her laughing by herself in the boys' room. After a little she appeared in the garb of Nesto – but what a Nesto! Those were his trousers but on Ilde they had become enormous and loose, and that was his working-shirt, all patched although freshly laundered, but it looked like a circus clown's.

'Come on, let's dress up too!' the others shouted in great excitement, gathering round Ilde.

They ran in and turned the boys' things topsyturvy – striped socks and linen shirts, Wehrmacht caps and English army blouses. When all five had dressed up they went down the stairs, pushing one another, out of breath, to show themselves to the old women.

To begin with the latter showed signs of disapproval but then began to laugh in the way only women laugh, covering their mouths like naughty girls and calling on the Lord.

But suddenly they told the young people to go back to their rooms and stop because 'there can be too much of a good thing'. But the girls did not even listen. They were like frisky foals. They went out into the courtyard which, with the last of the sun, was already again in the grip of a melancholy cold. The bigger ones wished to go to visit their friends they had just left and give them a surprise. But Cecilia and Ilde wanted to go on to the main road. They ended by squabbling and split up. When Cecilia and Ilde, on their own, ran on to the roadside the sun was setting behind the Carnic Alps. It just touched the rows of mulberries and the ruby-red osiers in tufts along the canal banks.

Suddenly, preceded by a confused noise of footsteps, music and voices, the procession of masks appeared from the San Floreano road. The carts, one shaped like a boat, one like a hut, one like a tower, came towards them dragging with them in the dust of the main road some pieces of evergreen, some broken stalks of maize. In front of the carts, worn out by the long trip, walked the people on foot, got up in the strangest ways, in patched sheets, sacks, old suits and peasant costumes and with undefinable rags wrapped round their shoulders. It was impossible to tell from the faces whether they were men or women because of the tattooing, the false moustaches and the untidy hair that came over their eyes.

Between one cart and the next, right to the back of the procession, these groups of people on foot were scattered, dragging their shoes in the dust which did not rise, as if it were sand.

Behind the first cart came the big heads two or three metres in diameter, which bobbed against the sky on the little legs of the persons who wore them, with gaping, laughing mouths, staring eyes surrounded by wrinkles and red, shiny cheekbones.

But all of them, almost in silence, walked in a tired way as if they could go no farther, even those dressed as women, who were the biggest and tallest and looked as if they were of the same stock as the prize-fighter Carnera.

Further back there was the cart with the orchestra and the players who every so often struck up without conviction, and further back still more big heads which rolled about with flapping ears like so many hanged men.

Cecilia and Ilde sat there in deeper silence, delighted to see the show from close at hand; they were all eyes, squatting with their dirty trousers on the short grass which was still warm from the sun, yellow as straw, with here and there the greenish colour of the first daisies.

They wore their caps low on their foreheads and had streamers scattered on their clothes, one green, one orange, one violet, one yellow. So they watched and did not move.

Very slowly the interminable procession, whose head had already turned in between the first houses at Rosa, almost came to an end. There was still a cart struggling along after the others and behind it a group of youths passing round a bottle and taking pulls at it. Now they could hear the songs of the people entering the village and the group of big heads, down there at the bend in the road, had begun to move up and down again. A curious need for haste came over the rearguard and a few words, a joke or two or a shout passed from mouth to mouth, their high spirits alight again.

Two or three youths, before quickening their steps towards the last spree in their own village, halted and, laughing, lined themselves up at the edge of the ditch just before the bank where Cecilia and Ilde were sitting; the air was almost dark and cold but still pervaded by a white glimmer of light. 'Well then, when's the confetti!' shouted one of the youths with a hoarse voice. 'Soon! Soon!' replied another. 'Soon, eh?' said the first. 'Has to be,' said the second, hoarse and almost shouting, 'she's pregnant!' Meanwhile all the youths, without taking any notice of the two dressed-up boys, who were blind with astonishment, began – as one of them said – to put some water into the ditch which had been dry since the winter. The one who was farthest behind and had shouted that he had to get married, after groping with his drunkard's hands in his trousers without success, took the enormous head from his shoulders and laid it on the side of the ditch. Thus above his white wool sweater his black wavy hair and his shining eyes reappeared. It was Nini, dead drunk, burnt up by the sun and the wine. He took his place in the row with the others to do the same thing, as disdainful and distracted as an animal, and taking a long time over it, as happens with drunks. And he did not even notice the two little peasant boys who had suddenly got up from the crushed grass of the bank and, with their old caps pulled down over their ears and coloured streamers fluttering round them, ran down along between the vines, shouting until their voices had died away beyond the rows.

What an effect it had on Ilde, each time she entered the bedroom, to see Cecilia's palliasse without sheets and wrapped in the tightly-stretched blankets. Although when she did the room she tidied it every morning along with her own it seemed that an invisible dust had been deposited on it for ever.

The light was sad even on fine days because the windows of the bedroom looked to the north, towards the mountains; but it seemed even sadder when it touched that empty palliasse, which was always so tidy.

Ilde looked at it as little as possible, especially in the evening, when she went to bed and it was so grey and neat beside her own. She knelt in front of the picture of the Sacred Heart with its two blessed sprigs of olive which were the only dusty thing in the little room and after saying her prayers slipped into her sheets without the merriment of old times.

On the other hand things had happened so fast that Ilde had not yet been able to get used to them. The summer was not even over, the grape harvest was in full swing, the little red apples of the orchard had just been gathered and laid out in the baskets. And when the apples, which were the property of the Faedis boys — since there were only four or five poor trees behind the dung-heap — were gathered Cecilia was still at home. She had gone with her other young brothers and cousins, through the fields which were joyfully green and red along the road which divided the cottage from the first fields to the little orchard. She had leant the rough ladder against the thin whitewashed trunks and had climbed up into the tough foliage among the little apples, which blushed, fresh and wild, little bigger than cherries. All the boys shouted and laughed round about in the familiar quiet and even the old grandfather had come out under the tree, dragging his slippers on the grass, mixed with hay and spattered with whitewash, to sit on the edge of the trough that watered the garden. Every so often an adult came by to help harvest these homely apples but in reality to laugh a little with the young people. But Cecilia already had about her a new air, something a little mysterious, and very different from normal — a slightly starched air, as if she were too pure, pious and submissive, a little like the nuns at the children's home. She too laughed and played with the others but there was about her presence in the house a kind of detachment, a distance which made Ilde and the other children feel a sort of shyness and at the same time a special tenderness.

It had all begun with tears and desperate weeping, with a pain no one understood; it had actually begun to separate Cecilia from her family and to isolate her, as if something had descended upon her, something which no longer had anything in common with the Faedis and everyday life.

No one had noticed anything. The chatter and the innocent jokes of the other girls about Nini had gradually stopped just as they had begun and no one even remembered them any more, so much so that the day Nini and Pia were married, which was in May at the first mowing of the hay, when they passed in their little cart along with their friends and relatives, right in front of the Faedis' cottage, no one even thought of Cecilia who stood there watching with the others with her hoe in her hand, hot and smiling gently among the first mown hay.

She had kept everything to herself, had done everything herself; only the priest and Sister Celeste, her favourite nun, knew something. She left soon after the apples were gathered on a September day – oh, not to go very far but it seemed like the end of the world. The mother house of the Sisters of the Sacred Heart where she was going for her novitiate was at Vittorio Veneto. But for some time she had had in her expression, in her way of doing things, in her bearing in church or at home, the same air as the nuns and seemed out of place in that old countryside of the Faedis, red, blue, dark-green, overflowing with maize, with the vines bending under the weight of the grapes. The men, particularly the young ones, were almost estranged from her. When she left, the cart – the old one with the very big black wheels, as high as a throne, with its rough curved sides – was full of girls: Cecilia, in the middle on the high seat, with a bundle at her feet and all round sisters and cousins. Only Nisiuti, the smallest of the family, who had grown into a big boy, was on the front seat with the whip in his hand and his blond quiff over his fiery red forehead.

At his shout Marco, the horse he had played with so much as a child, pawed the beaten earth of the courtyard in the middle of the circle of members of the family in their best black clothes who were shouting and waving goodbye. The horse went through the gate, left the big walnut-tree behind, the pump, the black group of relatives in the doorway, and turned down the main road towards San Floreano. The Faedis' cottage disappeared behind the vines and the thickets which grew along the canal. In the midst of the great sea of green with red and blue wild flowers spilt over the fields, there was the great silence of a summer afternoon. All that could be heard clearly was the song of the nightingale among the thickets and Cecilia's low weeping.

They passed along the long main road, passed San Floreano with its big square on the canal and the inn, passed between tunnels of green along the road with all the bends that led to Casarsa. And there were the first walls of Casarsa, stone walls, discoloured with smoke, beside the tarred road; here was Borgo Pordenone with its old, narrow house-fronts, its big arcades, peasants coming back with carts full of hay, a few soldiers, a few gentlemen of the kind one never saw at Rosa; and finally the new station in the square, which was white with dust and whitewash, silent as a lazaretto.

On the station steps there were the two nuns waiting for Cecilia, all anxious and sweating. The cart drew up in front of them and Nisiuti got down to give the horse some hay, quickly so that he could enjoy the sight of the station, of the bar, of the trains. The whole group of girls and nuns went into the station entrance, which was empty and as hot as a furnace, to wait, patient and worried.

After some time the station bell finally began to ring; as if spirited away, dragging their baggage, the nuns and Cecilia ran towards the gate with all the girls behind them, crowding round the barrier, and the lame ticket-collector laughing and very pleased with himself.

'Goodbye, goodbye,' they all cried together. But Cecilia did not turn round, being alarmed, as were the nuns, at the arrival of the train which was coming in with a tremendous din. They saw her climb up into an old third-class coach among the faces of schoolchildren and workers and disappear into a compartment with her long skirts of grey cotton.

'Goodbye, Cecilia!' they continued to shout to her, especially Ilde, who was weeping like someone distraught. Then the express slowly started to move. It was already going fast when it reappeared beyond the building, beyond the level-crossing, towards the bend that led to Pordenone.

XII

It was not Eligio, this boy lying in the little bed in the ward. The ravaged face, the long hair, the shoulders sticking out of the sheets, seemed those of a child of thirteen.

Rather than white, his skin was of a colour that had no name, that of entrails which have never seen the light of day; on the gleaming sheets there was a sort of yellow spot, only lighter than that, where one could no longer distinguish the lips, far less the pupils of the eyes, which had become pale and opaque and had also taken on the colour of meat. The bones of his face stuck out, lengthening it from the cheekbones to the chin. Perhaps it was this that had disfigured Eligio to the point where he was unrecognizable, but above all it was his eyes. He threw glances here and there, it is true, as if he was looking for a way out, a known face, but these were merely movements of the pupils which no longer had any consciousness.

Sometimes he let his arms fall along the sides of the child's body on the blankets; sometimes he raised them in his delirium, and waved them about, shaking his head. Sometimes in his anguish he struck with his closed fist at the wall against which his little iron bed stood.

It was this spasmodic gesture that, with unconscious obstinacy, he repeated most often. He looked for a moment into the eyes of those who were around him, then turned his head away and began to punch the wall anew. It was night and along the ward, under the lights, the other sick people were trying to sleep.

123

They were all poor – on their wrinkled faded faces there was imprinted the sadness of poverty rather than illness; a life passed in the fields, on a bed of maize-husks, at the greasy table of an inn, by a hearth shared with hostile relatives. Now they had been brought here, laid out on these beds and left to lie there with their illness. In their eyes there remained only an expression of selfishness and of astonishment. No one turned towards the bed where Eligio was dying. Not even the relations and friends gathered round him could arouse any interest. In the ward, which was really a windowless and airless corridor, into which they were packed, these were things that happened every day. It was thus that the poor were destined to die.

For hours on end Eligio did not recognize anyone then suddenly for a while he seemed to come to himself. Then his father or Onorino, who for some days now had become aware of this, came closer to him and asked if he needed anything. He looked at them for a moment and said some unrecognizable words like a child that has just learned to speak. In reality he did not say anything and mixed together a confusion of syllables with a kind of sigh or yawn, as if he found the effort unbearable.

Nini and Milio came and, as soon as they entered, sat by the bedside. Old Pereisson rose and the two friends went to shake his hand. 'It's all over now,' said the old man and Onorino looked at the two of them with terror. 'Doesn't he recognize anyone any more?' asked Nini. 'Yes,' said the old man, 'every so often.' Nini went up to Eligio, bending over the bed. He lay still and looked at him with his eyes wide open on a ravaged face. Then suddenly he turned away, waving his arm in a tired gesture, punching the wall in his delirium. 'Eligio,' called Nini. He did not hear him and continued to rub his cheek on the pillow and to punch the wall. Nini looked at Eligio again. His lips and gums were dry and pale, the skin cracked. He had no more fever and was cold now. Nini stood so close that their breaths almost mingled. He put a hand on his shoulder too, calling his name. But Eligio did not recognize him. He continued to make his delirious gestures as if he were in the grip of a terrible anxiety.

'The doctor says,' Onorino murmured, 'that it can go on like this a long time.' Nini looked at him. The boy had spoken calmly, looking fixedly at him with eyes in which he could read an anguish more powerful than anything he could imagine.

'Ah, let's hope not, let's hope not,' said the father. 'It's better for him to die quickly if he has to die.'

'But maybe he will live,' exclaimed Nini.

'Oh yes,' said Milio naïvely.

But the old man, without speaking, leaned over his son. 'Eligio,' he shouted. 'Eligio, look who has come to see you.'

Eligio did not hear him, locked in the agony by which he was consumed. With immobile arms he slowly shook his head, pressing it hard against the pillow. 'Eligio!' cried Milio. 'It's no use,' said the old man shaking his head. 'Sit down for a little, comrades.'

Nini sat down. Milio leant on the side of the bed. 'Ah,' said old Pereisson, 'he had been ill for so long!' 'Yes, I knew,' said Nini, 'but why didn't he get treatment?' 'He went to the doctor once,' said the father, 'but they couldn't find anything. And he went on going to the quarry. When I saw him getting thinner every day till he was almost a skeleton I said to him: "Don't go to the quarry any more, Eligio." But he began to laugh. "And what about the shoes for Onorino and the apron for Mother — what am I to buy them with?" he said. He went on working until one day at the quarry he fell ill and his mates brought him home.'

Try as they might, the two friends could not imagine how that body could be the body of Eligio. They had nothing in common. Of the sparkling light blue of the eyes there was no trace nor of that intense, fixed smile — the smile of the evening at Casale, for example, when he had started to sing in English with the broom for a guitar, inventing the words, or that evening when he had seized the flag from its corner behind the cupboard and had waved it over the heads of the comrades.

This little parchment face, this little white nightshirt which covered his thin body to the chin, but above all this cold fever of his, which made him stretch his arms with a gesture like a child or an animal, turned him into something so defenceless, so weak, that pity for him was stronger than the very pain of seeing him die.

Milio leant with his elbows on the edge of the bed. He was wearing his loose white jacket bought with the money from Switzerland, which he treated with great care and wore on special occasions. He looked at Eligio with the same expression as Onorino. Every so often he distracted himself by watching what went on round about — a nun passing, a patient who was already convalescent getting up by himself and slowly putting on his shoes. Half an hour later Alba, Eligio's elder sister, came in with two or three other acquaintances from San Giovanni. Without saying anything they came round the bed to look at the invalid. He continued to rave and to sigh out a few incomprehensible words, unable to stay still for a minute. Now he thrust out his sharp chin, stretching his neck; now he pressed his cheek hard on the pillow as he had been doing all day.

'Eligio,' said his sister, almost weeping, 'look at me, I am Alba.' He glanced at her. 'Yes,' he said. Everyone drew closer.

'He understands,' murmured Nini, looking at the father, who leant over Eligio, calling his name and shaking him by the arm: 'Son,' he said. 'Look how many people have come to see you.' 'Yes, so many,' said Eligio, almost distinctly, like a child who is having a birthday and timidly shows its gratitude. Nini drew closer and Eligio's father and brothers made way for him near the sick man as if the friend had the greater right. But Eligio seemed unable to recognize him. 'How are you?' asked Nini. 'Ah, well,' the boy replied in his agony. Eligio begin to turn his head to and fro again and to hit the wall. 'You must get better, you know, Eligio,' said Nini leaning over and almost touching his brow with his hand. Eligio nodded. 'Hey, comrade, don't you remember me?' asked Nini. Eligio turned his head towards him almost at once and quickly murmured an incomprehensible phrase with an effort so extreme that it left him breathless with his eyes shut. He went on shaking his head as if to show that he knew who Nini was, then he gazed at him fixedly for some time. It seemed as if something like a smile was born deep in his dim eyes. Suddenly he pointed a finger at Nini but his arm fell immediately as he once more said some senseless words and groaned. 'Something,' he seemed to be saying, 'something!' And he was referring to something almost as if he were winking, to something which he and Nini and Milio knew well. But he didn't speak, he didn't succeed in saying what it was. It was there in his eyes. He would not have been able to say it even when he was strong and full of life so what chance had he of managing to say it now that he was dying?

A few days later the courtyard at the Pereissons' was empty, swept, as on Sunday afternoons when the men have gone out – the old ones to the inn, the young ones, to who knows where in the nearby hamlets, and the women to Mass.

Piles of canes were gathered against the pillars of the lean-to shed, the faggots and the firewood in orderly heaps; not a leaf, not a husk on the edge of the runnel, which from the pump ran between the troughs in the courtyard and reflected its hard, white, sparse light which was like that of the clouded sky. Since there was not a breath of air the cold was hard and pitiless. Here in the open air, in the courtyard surrounded by the gardens and then, right behind them, by the fields, there was the silence of an abandoned church. The ramshackle windows of the families who lived in the same courtyard as the Pereissons were barred above their empty balconies. But the silence from time to time was made deeper by the sound of the bells which awoke high up with muffled, distant peals.

In the courtyard, all around, some dozens of people were standing and in the Pereisson house one heard quiet movements, blows and bumps without echo, as if someone were climbing or descending the little wooden stairs. The little gate in front of the kitchen door was open and, in fact, every so often someone went in to see Eligio on his bed and came out soon after with his hat in his hand and his head bowed. They were almost all men in their best black suits. The women were gathered under the balcony which led to the Pereissons' attic and along the barn, hidden in their little black veils. Standing there they could distinctly hear sobbing – although it was muffled and distant. In the midst of a group of men – the young ones had almost all remained in the porch – there was Susanna talking quietly to Leon and Giovanni Blasut. Every so often they looked up towards the sky which was heavy with white clouds and threatened snow. Perhaps they were talking about the weather and the work in the fields. Then suddenly they left the group and with their caps in their hands crossed the threshold of Eligio's house. The kitchen, clean and sweet-smelling, seemed even bigger with its hearth in the

127

middle, black, discoloured but without a speck of ash and with the fire-dogs polished. Apart from the door there was only one window behind the hearth through which a desolate light entered. On the upper floor one did not come out by way of the balcony as in the other houses in the courtyard but by a little staircase which started at the shutterless door to a dusty whitewashed cellar, lit by a weak electric lamp, within it the wine casks, the demijohns, the sacks, the tyres. This was the house where Eligio had lived for twenty years. His bedroom was the little room over the cellar; it had a crust of whitewash, which had sprayed the black beams of the ceiling and the floor of rough, badly laid planks. His bed was old netting, resting on a couple of trestles and covered by a mattress filled with maize-husks, while that of Onorino, who slept with him, was simply a palliasse, also filled with husks. But now Eligio was not lying there in his bedroom but in that of his father and mother, which was the only one to have furniture – the furniture his parents had bought when they married and which they had kept with such care that it was still like new: a bed, a chest of drawers and two chairs. But the room was as big as a full-length attic; the furniture was lost in it and seemed poor and naked on the floor so clean and sweet-smelling. But near the door one saw a worm-eaten table on which had been placed a glass of water with a sprig of olive. The room was full of people crowding in silence round the bed in the chilly shadow. On entering Susanna and the other men took the wet sprig from the glass and with it traced in the air the sign of the cross.

A few minutes later some youths came running upstairs, almost noisily, to warn people that the priest was arriving. Almost everybody went back down into the courtyard where in the meantime the children from the home had already arrived, led by the nuns, and, clattering with their clogs on the pavement, lined up in front of the Pereissons' door around the little white banner which one of them gripped in little hands inflamed by the cold. And again the peals of the bells came, echoing against the bare walls of Romans. Shortly afterwards the priest walked quickly into the courtyard, followed by the little attendants. They disappeared into the dark kitchen and from somewhere in the house the sobbing burst out more loudly because the silence had deepened. The animals could be heard moving and breathing in the byre and some sparrows chirping in the orchard.

On either side of the door with its whitewashed lintel two little wreaths had been placed, dark, poor, with the colour of the flowers so dead that they could not be distinguished from the dark green of the leaves and the grey of the stones. While the people in the courtyard began to prepare to form up, speaking almost loudly, with a kind of relief, Onorino and Livo went up to one wreath and Cini and Ivano to the other in their light holiday clothes, red with cold, and tried to lift them and keep them steady. Inside the house noises could be heard — bumps, voices, the noise of people's feet coming down the stairs and suddenly, loud and near, the wailing of the mother who called on Eligio two or three times by name, while they carried the coffin, which had now been closed, downstairs.

It was Nini, Milio and the other comrades who bore it on their shoulders. They came slowly out into the courtyard, having carried it down the stairs with such difficulty, in silence, and behind them came the relatives and the friends of the family. The priest set off at once, followed by all the others, towards the big gate and, turning down along the Romans road, they moved towards the church.

QUARTET ENCOUNTERS

The purpose of this paperback series is to bring together influential and outstanding works of twentieth-century European literature in translation. Each title has an introduction by a distinguished contemporary writer, describing a personal or cultural 'encounter' with the text, as well as placing it within its literary and historical perspective.

Quartet Encounters will concentrate on fiction, although the overall emphasis is upon works of enduring literary merit, whether biography, travel, history or politics. The series will also preserve a balance between new and older works, between new translations and reprints of notable existing translations. Quartet Encounters provides a much-needed forum for prose translation, and makes accessible to a wide readership some of the more unjustly neglected classics of modern European literature.

Aharon Appelfeld · *The Retreat*

'A small masterpiece . . . the vision of a remarkable poet'
New York Times Book Review

Alain · *The Gods*

'There are not a few of us in the world who think Alain was, and remains, one of the greatest men of our time. I would not myself hesitate to say, the greatest'
André Maurois

Gaston Bachelard · *The Psychoanalysis of Fire*

'. . . he is a philosopher, with a professional training in
the sciences, who devoted most of the second phase of
his career to promoting that aspect of human nature
which often seems most inimical to science: the poetic
imagination . . .'
J.G. Weightman, *The New York Review of Books*

Robert Bresson · *Notes on the Cinematographer*

'[Bresson] is the French cinema, as Dostoyevsky
is the Russian novel and Mozart is German music'
Jean-Luc Godard, *Cahiers du Cinéma*

Hermann Broch · *The Sleepwalkers*

'One of the greatest European novels . . .
masterful' Milan Kundera

E.M. Cioran · *The Temptation to Exist*

'Cioran is one of the most delicate minds of real power
writing today. Nuance, irony, and refinement are the
essence of his thinking . . .' Susan Sontag

Stig Dagerman · *The Games of Night*

'One is haunted by a secret and uneasy suspicion
that [Dagerman's] private vision, like Strindberg's
and Kafka's, may in fact be nearer the truth of things
than those visions of the great humanists, such as
Tolstoy and Balzac, which people call universal'
Michael Meyer

Stig Dagerman · *German Autumn*

'[German Autumn] attracted, and still deserves,
attention, partly because [Dagerman] had a sharp eye for
concrete details, partly because he could argue
pungently, but mainly because he dared to see German

individuals as suffering human beings rather than simply
as tokens of national disgrace or guilt' Robin Fulton

Grazia Deledda · *After the Divorce*

'What [Deledda] does is create the passionate complex
of a primitive populace' D.H. Lawrence

Marcellus Emants · *A Posthumous Confession*

'Since the time of Rousseau we have seen the growth
of the genre of the *confessional novel*, of which
A Posthumous Confession is a singularly pure example.
Termeer [the narrator], claiming to be unable to keep
his dreadful secret, records his confession and leaves it
behind as a monument to himself, thereby turning a
worthless life into art' J.M. Coetzee

Carlo Emilio Gadda · *That Awful Mess on Via Merulana*

'One of the greatest and most original Italian novels
of our time' Alberto Moravia

Andrea Giovene · *Sansevero*

'Some novels can be flirted with, others constitute a brief
affair. Occasionally one is lured into a long marriage,
when the early tensions and subsequent *longueurs*
stabilize at last into a solid relationship. So it is reading
The Book of Giuliano Sansevero. One can see why, on
its way to this country . . . its author has been
compared with Proust and Lampedusa' *Daily Telegraph*

Martin A. Hansen · *The Liar*

'[The Liar] is both a vindication of religious truth
and a farewell to the traditional modes of extended
fiction. It is haunted by literary ghosts, and English
readers will recognize the shadowy forms of Hans
Anderson . . . and Søren Kierkegaard' Eric Christiansen

Eugene Ionesco · *Fragments of a Journal*

'I am not too sure whether I am dreaming or
remembering, whether I have lived or dreamt it.
Memories quite as much as dreams arouse in me the
strongest feelings of the unreality and the ephemerality
of the world . . .'
Eugene Ionesco, *Present Past, Past Present*

Gustav Janouch · *Conversations with Kafka*

'I read it and was stunned by the wealth of new material . . .
which plainly and unmistakably bore the stamp of Kafka's
genius' Max Brod

Ismaïl Kadaré · *The General of the Dead Army*

'Ismaïl Kadaré is presenting his readers not merely
with a novel of world stature — which is already a
great deal — but also, and even more important, with
a novel that is the voice of ancient Albania herself,
speaking to today's world of her rebirth' Robert Escarpit

Miroslav Krleža · *On the Edge of Reason*

'Paris had its Balzac and Zola; Dublin, its Joyce;
Croatia, its Krleža . . . one of the most accomplished,
profound authors in European literature . . .'
Saturday Review

Pär Lagerkvist · *The Dwarf*

'A considerable imaginative feat'
Times Literary Supplement

Valery Larbaud · *Fermina Marquez*

'As a psychological study of male adolescence it is
delicate, touching, unsentimental; the atmosphere of the
school is evoked with an unforgettable nostalgic
vivacity' Francis Wyndham

Osip Mandelstam · *The Noise of Time*

'Clarence Brown's translation of Mandelstam not only gives English readers the greatest twentieth-century stylist in Russian but is also one of the finest examples ever of the translator's art: a miracle of accuracy, tone and feeling of period' Guy Davenport

Henry de Montherlant · *The Bachelors*

'One of those carefully framed, precise and acid studies on a small canvas in which French writers again and again excel' V.S. Pritchett

Stratis Myrivilis · *Life in the Tomb*

'*Life in the Tomb* has moments of great literary beauty and of more than one kind of literary power. In 1917, Myrivilis was twenty-five. "Before I entered the trenches I had not the slightest inkling of life's true worth. From now on, however, I shall savour its moments one by one . . ." ' Peter Levi

Pier Paolo Pasolini · *A Dream of Something*

'. . . indisputably the most remarkable figure to have emerged in Italian arts and letters since the Second World War' Susan Sontag

Luigi Pirandello · *Short Stories*

'The outer world of Pirandello's stories – the appearance of its reality – has a deceptive monotony and a deceptive variety. The monotony is the mask which society exacts from us; the variety is the pathetic series of fragmentary masks in which we strut about the world' Frederick May

D.R. Popescu · *The Royal Hunt*

'Popescu's style may be compared to that of Gabriel
García Márquez in *One Hundred Years of Solitude*,
although it is more concrete and somewhat sharper . . .'
J.E. Cottrell and M. Bogdan

Rainer Maria Rilke · *Rodin and other Prose Pieces*

'[Rilke's] essay remains the outstanding interpretation
of Rodin's œuvre, anticipating and rendering otiose
almost all subsequent criticism'
William Tucker, *The Language of Sculpture*

Rainer Maria Rilke · *Selected Letters 1902–1926*

'By will-power and concentration, a sense of which is
immanent in all his letters, as if some great quiet animal
were crouching there, Rilke made himself into a great
European genius, probably the last of the breed' John
Bayley

Lou Andreas-Salomé · *The Freud Journal*

'Lou Andreas-Salomé was a woman with a remarkable
flair for great men and . . . it was said of her that she had
attached herself to the greatest men of the nineteenth
and twentieth centuries Nietzsche and Freud
respectively'
Ernest Jones, *The Life and Work of Sigmund Freud*

Stanislaw Ignacy Witkiewicz · *Insatiability*

'A study of decay: mad, dissonant music, erotic
perversion, . . . and complex psychopathic personalities'
Czeslaw Milosz